CHOP SHOP

CHOP SHOP

Season One

The Cadillac Job ty Stacy Woodson
Run and Gun by Joseph S. Walker
A Hunka Hunky Burning Rubber by Hugh Lessig
Barracuda Backfire by Tom Milani
Devin in the Rearview by Stephen D. Rogers
Here Comes the Judge by James A. Hearn
Billy Dinkin's Lincoln by John M. Floyd

TOM MILANI,
STEPHEN D. ROGERS,
JAMES A HEARN and JOHN M. FLOYD

CHOP SHOP

Season One, Volume 2

Series Created and Edited by
Michael Bracken

Down & Out Books
3959 Van Dyke Road, Suite 265
Lutz, FL 33558
DownAndOutBooks.com

The characters and events in this book are fictitious. Any similarity to real persons, living or dead, is coincidental and not intended by the author.

Cover design by Zach McCain

ISBN: 1-64396-399-6
ISBN-13: 978-1-64396-399-0

CONTENTS

Barracuda Backfire   3
Tom Milani

Devil in the Rearview   55
Stephen D. Rogers

Here Comes the Judge   101
James A. Hearn

Billy Dinkin's Lincoln   101
John M. Floyd

About the Editor   157

About the Authors   159

Car thieves and the chop shop that buys from them
combine to create high-octane stories of
hot cars, hot crimes, and hot times in Dallas, Texas.

BARRACUDA BACKFIRE

Tom Milani

1976

It was love at first sight.

Ten months after he bought the car, Billy Wright could recite the classified ad from memory:

1965 Plymouth Barracuda Formula S, Commando 273 cu. in. V8, 4 bbl. carb., medium blue metallic exterior, low mileage, one owner, must be seen to be believed.

The grainy black-and-white photograph offered little detail as to the veracity of the ad, but when Billy's father drove him to see the car, Billy simultaneously thought it was the most beautiful thing he'd ever laid eyes on and recognized that the "seen to be believed" part of the ad was less a lie and more a warning. The car needed work, and lots of it, but he wasn't deterred by the effort that would be required.

The owner, a square-jawed, buzz-cut man named Claudel Stevens, who to Billy's untrained eye looked anywhere from forty to sixty, bounced around the car, talking a mile a minute as he showed off the Edelbrock manifold, the wooden steering wheel, the interior that, with the back seat folded, could accommodate two people, as long as they were "close friends," he said with a wink.

Billy was trying to get a better look at the body when his father said, "Mr. Stevens, would you mind if my son and I spoke privately for a moment?"

"Of course, of course," he said, and disappeared around the side of the house.

Billy's father turned to him. "I know you have your heart set on this car. I confess I don't see the appeal, but cars are like women. What makes a girl attractive to you ain't the same as what makes her attractive to me."

Billy, almost seventeen years old and still a virgin, spent all his time thinking about two things: cars and girls, in that order. He was innocent, but he wasn't a fool. He turned to his father. "I was thinking of offering him five hundred less that what he's asking."

His father nodded. "I knew I raised you right."

Now the hood gleamed in the twilight, its reflection the product of hours of hand-rubbed Simonize. The V8 rumbled nicely. Sometimes Billy felt as if its power were part of him, that he was somehow a stronger, better person behind the wheel than he was separate from the car.

He didn't like sports, which marked him as a freak in a state as football-obsessed as Texas and a city as Cowboys-obsessed as Dallas. But his ability to work on cars was its own currency. Being able to adjust the fuel-air mixture on an aftermarket Holley four-barrel carburetor for someone with more money than sense tended to keep the bullies at bay.

Tonight he wore boot-cut Wranglers, a black Mopar T-shirt, and Tony Lama roach killers, which he got from a friend of his father's as payment for replacing a water pump. Freshly showered and shaved, he'd put on some of his father's Old Spice because Veronica liked the way it smelled on him. He parted his hair in the middle. In the mirror, Billy was lean like his father, but without his height; he had good skin, but ordinary features. Inside him was something more.

Billy drove south toward the Little Mexico neighborhood where Veronica lived in a small brick-front ranch with faded yellow trim. Wearing an embroidered sleeveless top, cutoffs, and turquoise ropers, she stepped out of her house and walked to the curb, where he was idling. Billy's heart lurched, the same as it had the first time he met her.

He'd been elbow deep in the engine bay of a Ford with a bad head gasket, tools resting on shop rags spread across both fenders, Bill Monroe playing on the cassette player in Farley's garage—music he claimed would help Billy work faster and smarter—when Veronica said, "Hello." Billy turned at the sound of her voice, which was lilting and warm.

It was love at first sight.

She had round cheeks, a dimpled chin, and a waterfall of dark, wavy hair framing her face. The strand of puka shells at her throat above her denim shirt set off her umber skin.

As she started to walk away, Billy, frozen in place, finally managed to speak.

"Hey," he said. "Do I know you?"

It was a stupid line, but he guessed he didn't come off as sleazy because her lips turned up in a smile, her eyes brightening.

"I see you here all the time working on Farley's truck, so I thought I'd say hi. What's wrong with it, anyway?"

"It's a Ford." Billy was a Mopar man. When Veronica didn't laugh, he went on. "Just lots of little things. Fuel pump. Brakes." He pointed to the engine. "Bad head gasket."

"You know how to fix all that stuff?"

"I'm learning," Billy said. "I check out books from the library, talk to people at Chief Auto. Some of the guys at the parts counter know everything, if you're willing to listen."

She tilted her head at him.

Billy wiped his hands on a shop rag. "What?"

"Most guys would have tried to tell me how smart they were about cars."

Billy shook his head. "There's so much to learn. Every time I think I've got a handle on a repair, something pops up." He shrugged. "But that's what I like about the work—there's always a challenge."

Now Veronica's smile broadened. "So, you like a challenge?"

Billy wasn't sure where this was going, but he smiled back and took her words as an invitation.

"My name's Billy Wright," he said, extending his hand.

She took it, her touch electric. "Veronica Valdez. Pleased to meet you."

"Likewise." Emboldened with a courage he usually lacked when it came to girls—and for once not overthinking things—he said, "You should go out with me."

She crossed her arms. "I should, should I?" Her voice was serious again.

"I mean, would you like to go out with me?"

"That's better, Billy."

But it wasn't that simple. Farley, a friend of his father's, was the only white face on Veronica's block and maybe in her entire neighborhood. How he ended up in Little Mexico was a mystery Billy never attempted to solve, but his father told him to be careful when he went there because "Farley didn't have sense enough to live among his own kind."

Billy got the occasional side eye when he was working on Farley's truck, but no one ever confronted him. Asking Veronica out came with complications, despite her ready answer and his simple thrill that she'd said yes. So, when Billy mentioned that he was planning to take a girl out the following weekend, he was careful only to use Veronica's first name, his father's opinion of Mexicans not being much higher than his opinion of Blacks. From the vantage point of the Old East Dallas block where he and his father lived, Billy saw little to lord over anybody, black or brown, but he kept those thoughts to himself.

For the first time in what felt like forever, he had a reason to believe in the future.

2021

Huey's Auto Repair was in an industrial park off Harry Hines.

Whenever he took his Jeep there, Billy always felt like he was driving into the past or, if not the past, a place where the progress that had so changed downtown Dallas and the surrounding suburbs over the last twenty years appeared to simply bypass Huey's and every other nearby business.

Billy wasn't quite a Luddite—he had an iPhone, his one indulgence in a life otherwise spartan in its creature comforts—but at some point, cars became too complicated and uninteresting for him to work on. They had black boxes in place of components you could actually see; repair became less rebuild and more replace. More than that, he was too old to be crawling under his Jeep, trying to fix whatever was wrong with its front end.

He found Huey's a few years ago, after getting the runaround from two dealers with their diagnostics and calls to corporate that somehow never seemed to provide a lasting fix for the Jeep's intermittent electrical problems. Leticia—Tish—Huey's service manager, said it was a poor ground in two places. The bill was a good deal higher than he expected—the job being a by-the-hour diagnosis, so she couldn't even give him an estimate beforehand—but he hadn't complained, grateful there were still competent mechanics around.

Still, it was more than Tish's competence that warmed her to Billy. Her voice and accent were a dead ringer for Veronica's. If he closed his eyes, he could swear it was Veronica speaking, which meant, in a way more concrete than the memories that came and went, she was still present in his life.

Ahead, two van drivers yelled at each other, their vehicles' bumpers forming a chevron where they'd collided, the drivers' Eastern-European-accented English suggesting grievances held for generations. Rather than attempting to inch his way around them, Billy turned left, assuming he could cut back on a parallel street and find his way to Huey's.

But here this section of road wound in a lazy arc, and he lost track of the grid. When he finally turned, nothing looked familiar. Never one for going back, he took a right on a street heading in what he thought was the general direction of the shop, but a half mile later it became an alley that narrowed at a lot marked by cyclone fencing topped with barbed wire. Billy stopped, curious.

He got out of his Jeep and stood on the running board. Inside the fence, cars and trucks were parked in rows, none of them whole, and he guessed the lot held vehicles being stripped for their parts. He couldn't see any sign for the business, but beyond all the vehicles, part of a building was visible. He recognized the white sides and blue trim and realized he was directly behind Huey's. On other visits, he'd glimpsed the back lot when the front and rear bay doors were opened, but he had no sense of its scale.

A truck headed toward him. Over the clatter of its diesel, Billy heard the rattle of an automatic gate sliding open, and the truck, a flatbed with a car strapped to it, turned into Huey's lot.

Billy's mouth went dry, and his heart galloped in his chest. Even at this distance, he recognized his Barracuda, starting with the S badge on the rear quarter panel; moving to the chrome bumpers, wheel covers, and trim he'd polished till his hands cramped; and ending at the metallic blue paint, which he'd applied in layers until it looked like White Rock Lake under the summer sun.

The flatbed's course wound through the yard until it disappeared inside the maze of junked cars. Billy drove past the lot, his mind blank save for one thought: he had to get his car back.

1976

"Billy, this is so beautiful."

He walked Veronica around the Barracuda, which he'd finished waxing about an hour earlier. The silver stripes bisecting the hood appeared like streaks of moonlight. He even showed her the engine because he was proud of all the work he'd done on it.

"For a while, I wasn't sure if it even existed," she said. "You should have let me see it earlier."

"It needed a lot of work," he said. "I wanted to surprise you."

"Consider me surprised." She squeezed his arm.

Veronica lived with her tía. Louisa and Veronica were both about five-four, but Louisa was stout, her round features rarely forming a smile, at least when Billy was around. He tried to win her over by working on her car, not even charging her for parts. Tía Louisa didn't exactly warm to Billy, but after he'd replaced her fuel pump so that the engine purred instead of sputtered, she gave him an extra piece of flan, saying he needed to eat more. He respected her for raising Veronica as her own. Veronica had never met her father, and her mother was somewhere in Mexico. Billy couldn't remember his own mother, he'd been so young when she died. His father wouldn't talk about her. That gave Billy and Veronica something in common and spared them awkward questions of each other.

Now, he shut the door after she dropped into the Barracuda's passenger seat, but not before taking a longing look at her brown legs, visions of which had begun invading his dreams.

Billy pulled away from the curb. Veronica waved to her tía, who didn't wave back. He kept the rear seats folded down, and in the back carried a blanket and some tools. Tonight, he also had a cooler with a six-pack of Lone Star, courtesy of Farley, who told Billy, "the course of true love never did run smooth," adding that a beer or two might help it run smoother.

Billy didn't see the point of getting stinking drunk on weekends like some of his classmates bragged they did, but a little buzz to calm his nerves couldn't hurt. It helped that the day was mild for the Fourth of July in Texas. The clouds kept the heat down, and the breeze fluttered Veronica's hair as Billy's own fingers sometimes did. Feeling bold, he squeezed her thigh, her smooth skin warm to his touch. When he returned his hand to the steering wheel, his palm felt imprinted with the contours of her leg.

At Fair Park they held hands, getting a few dirty looks from people who'd come there for the Bicentennial celebration, but Billy told himself he didn't care.

"I don't know, Billy," Veronica started, looking at the crowd. "Maybe this wasn't such a good idea."

The grounds teemed with people, and suddenly it felt like a party gone bad. "Don't you want to watch the fireworks?" he asked, trying to mask his own discomfort.

"Can we go somewhere else?"

He shrugged and turned around. In the parking lot he'd backed into a spot facing the Cotton Bowl. Veronica giggled when he motioned to the folded seats but scurried into the back. He followed, pulling the door shut behind him. He bunched the blanket like a pillow, and they lay next to each other, the Barracuda's wraparound rear glass like a window to the clouds above them.

When the fireworks began, the sound of their explosions was muted by the car, but the colored starbursts spangling the night sky seemed magnified by the glass. Holding Veronica's hand, he felt his heart race, its beating somehow amplified by the percussion above.

When the show ended, Veronica said, "That was beautiful."

He rolled to her, and she met him. They kissed slowly, and Billy pressed a hand on the embroidery of her shirt, feeling her breast beneath. His head spun until Veronica pushed his chest.

"We can't, Billy. Not here."

The "not here" portion of what she said spurred him to action. Veronica laughing, he threw himself over the front seat. He got out of the car and helped her from the back.

As he drove them to White Rock Lake, "American Pie" came on the radio, and Veronica cranked the volume. Billy didn't know exactly what the song meant, but he knew all the words, and the chorus was easy to sing along to. At one point he stopped and listened as Veronica sang, her eyes closed and head thrown back, her alto tones rich and full, filling Billy's heart with a love he didn't know he was capable of feeling.

He'd been fishing at White Rock Lake ever since he could bait his own hook. His father took him there, taught him how to cast and gut a fish. Sometimes Farley was with them. On those days, he and his father would drink beer as Billy fished. When he got older, his father would drop him off Saturday mornings and pick him up late in the afternoon, and that night he would cook whatever Billy had caught. After he earned his driver's license, Billy cruised around the lake in his truck, a beater that barely ran, watching girls, checking out cars. Lots of kids hung out in the park, but some days it got out of hand, and people who lived off Lawther Drive complained. He envied guys walking with their girlfriends, which always seemed a world just beyond his grasp.

With Veronica sitting next to him now, he told himself he was like those guys, but something kept him from believing it.

They parked on a dirt path Billy knew about from fishing. Veronica reached for him, and they kissed, the steering wheel pressed against his side. After they pulled apart, Billy whispered, "Do you want to go in the back?"

"Yeah, Billy, I do."

The view through the wraparound window was all shadows, the starless sky mottled shades of gray. In the distance engines revved, but nothing neared them. They kissed again while unbuttoning and untucking and unzipping, and soon Billy felt the rough fabric he'd scrubbed clean against his shoulder blades and Veronica's small, smooth breasts against his chest.

He ran his hands the length of her body, and she held him with a strength he didn't know she possessed.

"Did you bring any protection?"

He found his jeans and fished through the pockets for his wallet, where he had a single condom. As he unwrapped it, Veronica's sigh of relief seemed an invitation.

When he entered her, she cried out, and he froze. "Are you all right?"

She squeezed his back and shifted her hips. "It's okay."

As he found his rhythm, Veronica wrapped her legs around

him, and he rose, lifting her with him, all his muscles contracted like a fist. When he came, he felt as if time had stopped, he and Veronica somehow existing outside this mortal coil. He eased them both down and lay next to her, his chest rising and falling as his heartbeat finally slowed.

"We should have waited, Billy."

"What—why?"

"My tía says it's a sin."

Billy didn't know much about sin other than it seemed the natural order of things. "Even if I love you?" he asked.

In answer, Veronica climbed on top of him and kissed him. He shifted his weight, and soon he was hard again. "I don't have another—"

"Shh," Veronica said, taking him into her mouth. When she inched a finger inside him, his breath caught and he closed his eyes, losing himself in a wave of pleasure and pain.

Afterwards, Billy opened two of the Lone Stars, and they sat crossed-legged, facing the rear of the car, Billy's arm around Veronica's shoulders. He felt relaxed and unsettled, the two emotions alternating as her weight shifted against him.

"We should head back," Veronica said, and began dressing. Billy watched her awhile before putting on his own clothes. They didn't say much on the drive home, and as soon as he pulled up to Veronica's house, her tía was in the doorway, glaring at Billy. Veronica squeezed his hand before running up the walk.

He came home to a dark house. The next day, as he was cleaning out the back of the Barracuda, he saw that the condom he'd worn was torn. He figured it happened when he took it off; he was sure he would have noticed otherwise.

2021

"Billy, are you okay?" Tish asked. "You look like you just saw a ghost.

He blinked and shook his head, realizing he'd simply been staring at the service desk, not even seeing Tish and unable to think about anything other than his Barracuda in Huey's back lot.

"Sometimes I think there's ghosts all around," he said. Billy looked at the Semper Fi tattoo running down Tish's right forearm, which she wouldn't talk about, and figured she'd seen a few ghosts of her own.

"What can I do you for today?" she asked.

"Look at the front end, would you? It's clunking on the right side and bounces me around every time I hit a bump."

Billy handed her the keys, and Tish said she'd call once they knew what work needed to be done.

Even if they weren't in the middle of a pandemic, Billy could never stand to sit in the waiting room, watching HGTV or ESPN, depending on who had the remote that day. Outside, the spring air was warming, the sky clear. Billy wore a jean jacket, and he sucked in his stomach as he unbuttoned it. He'd put on weight around his middle, but the rest of him was as ropy and lean as he'd been in high school. Until he saw his car being brought into Huey's lot, he resisted dwelling on the past, memory's potholed and broken road leading him only to a bad place. Now, however, he couldn't stop the visions that flooded his consciousness like a collage—Veronica's small breasts, narrow waist, and hips with a swell to them; her tawny skin and topaz eyes; the taut feel of her shoulders and the long muscles of her thighs. And beyond all that, the simple way her face lit up when she smiled at him. He couldn't think of the Barracuda without thinking about Veronica, and now that he knew the Barracuda existed, he wanted to find out what happened to her.

Her neighborhood was gone, the home she grew up in part of a highway median now. Even when they dated, road construction had begun pushing through the streets like a bulldozer, eminent domain forcing people out of their houses, many relocating into South Dallas. Over the ensuing decades, his own block had gone from poor white to poor black in a different sort of migration.

Billy understood how long-dead Farley must have felt living on Veronica's street—tolerated without being welcomed—but like Farley, he was indifferent to his neighbor's attitudes.

He found a food truck a few blocks away, the guy running it wearing a mask with the Texas state flag on it.

"¿Qué tal?" Billy said.

"Bien, gracias."

He ordered a green chile burrito and coffee and took them to a line of jersey barriers set randomly at the edge of the parking lot. As he ate, he imagined climbing into his car, starting the engine, and driving it out of Huey's. He still had a key for the Barracuda on the ring that held his house key. The idea was crazy, he knew, but he couldn't let it go.

Just as he couldn't let go of the idea of finding Veronica. For all he knew, she had grandkids, a still-handsome husband, and a brand-new Ford Super Duty in the garage. But so what if she did? It wasn't anything to hold against her. Billy would settle for hello and a hug and a few minutes of conversation to tell her how sorry he was and how he never stopped loving her. It was the stuff of a country song, he supposed, but that didn't make it any less true.

He crumpled the burrito wrapper and pitched it into an oil drum. Still carrying his coffee, he wandered through parking lots, recognizing the intersection that led to the road behind Huey's. He wasn't sure why the Barracuda was there. He didn't suppose it was for sale—not that he could have afforded it anyway. From what he'd glimpsed of it on the flatbed, the Barracuda was still cherry, so it wasn't going to be stripped for parts. The car didn't have the value of a Mustang or Corvette from the same era or of later Mopar muscle cars like the Challenger and Charger. It took someone like Billy to recognize the real beauty of the Barracuda.

Over the years he'd heard rumors about Huey's "other" business and about Huey himself, but Billy had never seen him in anything other than a dark suit, white shirt without a tie, and ropers that cost north of four figures. Billy always thought he looked like a cowboy undertaker, but until now, he hadn't considered that he might be one who also supplied the bodies he buried.

His phone rang, Tish's name on the display. "What's the damage?" he said.

"Your ball joints are shot. Supply chain the way it is, it might be a couple of weeks till we have them. You're okay waiting—as long as you don't take any corners too fast, the Jeep is safe to drive."

"At my age, I don't do anything fast anymore."

"All right, we'll call you when the parts are in."

That suited Billy fine. By then, he hoped to be long gone, miles of highway behind him, miles of open road ahead. He knew it was a fantasy. Even if he somehow took the Barracuda, he didn't have enough money to go far, and he had no idea how to disappear. He'd lived in the same house his entire life, his travels not extending more than a hundred miles in any one direction. Still, he felt the pull of his old car, as strong as gravity, as strong as love.

1976

"It's not fair the way the city treats Hispanics," Veronica said. "Do you think they'd put a highway through a rich white neighborhood?"

Billy didn't know anything about politics or politicians, but he thought they wouldn't hesitate to bulldoze a poor white neighborhood for the same purpose.

He shrugged. "The tornado that tore through North Dallas at the end of May didn't discriminate."

"Great, Billy. So, you're saying because God's not a bigot, everything's okay?" She started buttoning her shirt.

Her tía was at work, and they had been making out in Veronica's bedroom. Billy had gotten as far as second base when construction noise a few blocks away set her off. He didn't understand why what was going on with local politics was so important to her. As far as he was concerned, the situation was like the weather—you just tried to make the best of it.

"I'm sorry," he said, which he figured couldn't hurt.

Veronica leaned her head on his shoulder. "I'm not mad at you. I just hate feeling there's nothing I can do."

Billy felt that way about most things, except cars, which he could fix, and Veronica, whom he loved.

"Maybe someday you can," he said, his words emerging without conscious thought.

Veronica sat up and faced him. "My tía is always pushing me to go to college. I never took the SATs, but maybe I could go to El Centro in the fall."

Billy had one more year of high school left, but the idea of going to any college was as foreign as traveling to Mars. He figured he'd get a mechanic's job somewhere—show them the Barracuda, say I did all *this,* and let them make him an offer.

"Why not?" Billy said. "You're smart, and it's something you care about."

Veronica took his face in her hands and kissed him.

"Thank you."

Billy slid a hand under her shirt.

"My tía will be home soon. You'd better go."

Billy tapped his head against the wall and sighed. "Okay."

They kissed again, and he hustled out the front door. Billy drove to the end of block where Farley lived. He was kind of an honorary uncle to Billy—he couldn't remember a time when he wasn't around. He and his father could fix anything and often worked together on jobs. They looked like older and younger brother, Billy's father half a head taller than Farley, both of them with thinning hair, Farley's crew-cut. Mostly, they preferred drinking beer and fishing to working. Billy parked and Farley waved him inside.

At five-ten, Farley was two inches taller than Billy, but no heavier. Shirtless, his arms and chest were as worn and lined as gristle. Working in the sun had left him with tanned skin as brown as Veronica's, and he always seemed to be about a week from having last shaved.

"Want a beer? Help yourself, and grab one for me while you're at it."

Billy took a beer and a Mexican Coke from the refrigerator and followed Farley into his backyard. Two lawn chairs sat on a small slab of concrete. The weeds that poked through the dirt beyond looked like they'd be healthier underground.

"You come from your girl's place?" Farley asked.

Billy nodded. "She was complaining about the highway they're building."

"It's a damn shame," Farley said. "I'll probably have to sell."

"You will?"

Farley shrugged. "If I don't, they'll just take it."

Billy shook his head.

"You told your dad about her yet?"

"What's to tell? He knows I have a girlfriend."

"Billy, this is Farley you're talking to. You know your dad don't take kindly to Mexicans."

"Veronica is half-Mexican."

"Well, that's the half he's going to have a problem with."

"So why tell him?"

"Because you don't want him finding out from someone else. Because it means being a man, Billy."

"All right, I hear you." He wasn't looking forward to the confrontation, but he figured it would blow over fast. His father didn't seem to much care how Billy did in school or worry about what he did for fun. As far as Billy was concerned, his father had done the important things: taught him the basics of working on cars and that being your own boss was the key to happiness—though from what Billy could see, what that really meant was that Ernest Wright only worked when he wanted to.

"Your dad's a good man, but like all of us, he's got his blind spots. He did a fine job raising you, though."

Billy stood. "I should get going. Thanks for the Coke."

"Talk to your dad, Billy."

"I will."

"And bring your girl by sometime, I'd like to meet her." Before he could answer, Farley went on. "And I need you to take a look at the starter. It's acting up again."

"It's a Ford, is what you mean."

"Think of all the experience you're getting."

Billy just shook his head. This had definitely been his year for experiences, and so far, they'd all been good. He didn't see any reason why that couldn't continue.

2021

Inside his house the window unit struggled against the heat. Billy generally kept the A/C off but relented when the mercury pushed triple digits as it was this afternoon. He paced in the kitchen, too wound up to sit. Billy couldn't risk losing the Barracuda a second time. He had to go to Huey's tonight to scope out the security around the back lot and try to find his car.

Taking back the Barracuda—he couldn't use the word "stealing"—wasn't going to be easy, but Billy knew the hardest part was what happened after. He'd be on the run. Huey would announce a reward and, the Barracuda being as distinctive as it was, his phone would soon be ringing off the hook with people looking to collect. If Billy got lucky, he'd make it a hundred miles before Huey's people caught up to him.

What he really wanted was time behind the Barracuda's wheel again, Veronica by his side. He pulled out his phone. Billy preferred dealing with people in person, but the pandemic had forced him online. Once he got the hang of it, some things were easier. But not finding Veronica. He had done a search on her name and been overwhelmed by the number of matches in the

Dallas area alone. And that was assuming she hadn't married and changed her last name, which likely was wishful thinking on his part.

Billy tried to come up with something new. "Think," he said aloud. Billy remembered taking Veronica cruising on Forest Lane, north of Dallas. At the time, the street was famous for drag racing, and it was crowded on weekends. He felt proud driving the Barracuda, Veronica next to him, the windows down, Billy for once feeling like he belonged.

He shook his head at his younger self. Forty-five years ago most everyone kept with their own kind; forty-five years later the last president and his friends were blaming immigrants for all the country's problems. He thought what people called progress was an illusion necessary to keep the country from tearing itself apart. Too late.

He grabbed a Mexican Coke from the fridge and popped the top. A magnet with the Mopar logo held a postcard print of a Frida Kahlo self-portrait. Veronica gave it to him on his seventeenth birthday, her note on the back beginning *Querido Guillermo.* Billy liked Frida's eyebrows, which looked like they were getting ready to take off, and the flowers in her hair. Veronica told him about a Spanish-language biography of the artist written that year by a Mexican scholar who said Frida Kahlo was a feminist icon. At the time, he didn't understand what that meant or why it was so important to Veronica, but he was at least smart enough not to say so.

He typed Veronica Valdez Frida Kahlo into his phone, and on the third page of search results was a link to a Typepad blog. Billy clicked the link. Blowing up the thumbnail image in the top-left corner of her screen, he froze. It was Veronica. Billy bent over his phone as if it contained pages from a holy book and began reading the blog posts, working backwards from the last one in 2008. He read a few in their entirety but realized they didn't get him any closer to finding her. So, he continued clicking on the link for older posts until he reached the first.

There, Veronica introduced herself to her readers as a native Texan who now lived in Krum and was a lover of all things Frida. Billy figured Krum was about an hour away, give or take. Entries on her blog stopped thirteen years ago, so there was no telling whether she still lived there. He could search the property records online, but if she was a renter, she wouldn't show up.

What exactly was he doing here? he asked himself. In some recess of his mind, it occurred to Billy that Veronica had never tried to *find* him, which would have been easy for her. But before that thought could take root, he told himself she must have had reasons—good reasons—for never contacting him. What did matter was the here and now: Billy and his Barracuda, Billy and Veronica.

He found the property records for Denton, Texas, which included the outlying towns, and typed in her name, last name first, first name last, and waited for the result.

She was still there.

Her full name and address, details about the house's construction, the property value over the years, so much information he could picture the place just from the description. But because that wasn't enough, he copied and pasted the address into Google Earth to get a street view.

Here, things weren't as clear. Scrub trees hid the house, which was set back a good bit from the farm-to-market road, and there was no way to navigate any closer. As best as Billy could tell, Veronica must have been looking for the middle of nowhere and found it.

His mind spun as he tried to guess the reasons for her being there, but soon he calmed his thoughts. He could get answers to that and host of other questions, if she'd talk with him.

Billy lived day to day, not much taking stock of his life because he saw no upside to it. For the last forty-five years he'd followed in his old man's footsteps so closely you couldn't tell where Ernest Wright's footprints ended and where Billy Wright's began. A lifetime of odd jobs and no boss. True, unlike his father, he never married. But the women he'd slept with proved Billy's equal in terms of ambition, which was to say they had none. He knew where and when the best part of his life had been. If this was a fool's errand, so be it. He could no more imagine seeing Veronica again than he could driving the Barracuda, and he told himself both were within reach now.

He put the phone on the counter. On the screen, the two-lane road beckoned.

1976

Billy spread a blanket on the grass for him and Veronica. In the distance, White Rock Lake was the color of flatware, its surface solid and impenetrable.

Veronica wouldn't look at him. "I'm pregnant," she said.

Billy sucked in his breath, feeling as though he'd been punched in the gut.

"We used protection," she went on, facing him now. "I don't know what happened."

He did. "The condom tore, that first time. I thought it must have happened after, when I took it off."

Veronica's eyes went wide. "Billy—how could you not tell me?"

"I just said. I didn't think it was anything, just what happened after."

"What am I going to do?"

Billy noticed she didn't say "we."

"I'm not going anywhere." He spoke softly. The truth of his statement was self-evident—he had nowhere to go and no money to take him there—but behind that truth was a glimpse of their future, hazy in his mind's eye before today, now coalescing into something concrete.

"That's great, Billy. So, are we going to get married, live in our own apartment, raise our bebé?"

Billy hesitated.

"That's what I thought." Veronica turned away.

"Not all at once," he said. "I'd have to get a job first, save some money before we could afford our own place."

Veronica faced him again, her mouth open. "You're serious."

"Well, yeah."

"I've never even met your father, Billy. How's he going to react?"

Billy shook his head. "Not well." Farley had told him to talk to his dad, but the time never seemed right. Now he had no choice.

"Did you tell your tía?"

"I haven't told anyone. She's going to say I'm just like my mother."

Billy couldn't think of anything to say that would come across as other than a platitude. If he had to drop out of school to work full time, so be it. It wasn't like he was learning anything there anyway. He'd try for a mechanic's job but worried all he'd be able to get was a manual labor gig, minimum-wage work that would have to do until he got some experience.

He lay back on his elbows. Veronica looked at him over her shoulder.

"How are you so calm?" she asked. "This isn't a problem you can fix like an engine."

Billy's thoughts had been headed in that direction. "I'll talk to my dad tonight. Maybe he'll know who's hiring. We'll take it from there."

"Oh, Billy, it's not going to be that simple."

Farley had told Billy that filling his dad in about Veronica was part of being a man, but when they were sitting out back after dinner, Billy's father with a beer, Billy with a Mexican Coke, the words got stuck in his throat. He couldn't remember the last time they'd had a conversation involving anything more than whatever cars Billy was working on and whatever bullshit Ernest ran into on *his* jobs. Until he met Veronica, Billy thought that was just the natural order of things. But now he had no choice.

Finally, he spoke. "You know I've been seeing a girl," he started.

His father cocked an eyebrow. "Veronica, right?" he said.

Billy nodded and turned to his father. "Veronica Valdez."

His father's eyes narrowed, and the creases in his forehead deepened. Having gone this far, Billy figured it was time to rip the bandage.

"She's pregnant."

"How could you be so stupid?" his father asked, though the question was more of an accusation. "I do not want any beaner grandbabies."

Billy was stunned. Over the years he'd heard his father complain about Mexicans and Blacks, but those complaints seemed abstract—directed at whole groups of people—not aimed straight at Veronica, the girl Billy loved.

Billy stood. "Take that back."

His father lumbered from his chair and jabbed a finger at Billy's chest. "You've got no more sense than that stupid bitch who was your mother." His laugh was a sputter.

Anger boiling over, Billy swung his fist, but his father caught the punch in his left palm as if it were a baseball. He backhanded Billy with his right hand, the blow hitting his face like the side of a shovel and sending him sprawling to the yard. His eyes watered, and his head spun.

"Get out," his father said, the words low and rumbling. "Go play house with your girlfriend." He turned his back on Billy.

Billy wanted to throw himself at him, but his legs felt weighted down. In his bedroom, he tossed some clothes into his gym bag, having no idea what to take. When he came out of his bedroom, the house was empty, his father's truck gone.

Billy didn't have any friends he could stay with, and he didn't think Veronica's tía would like the idea of Billy living with Veronica any more than his father had, so he drove to Farley's, explained what happened, and asked if he could stay with him.

In answer, Farley said, "You need some ice for your face?"

Billy waved that off. "I'm fine."

"Your father will calm down after a few days."

Billy had his doubts. "Maybe."

"You can sleep in the den. The couch folds out, but the mechanism's sticky."

"I'll just sleep on it like it is," Billy said.

"That's what I'd do." Farley paced around the living room and into the kitchen. As far as Billy knew, Farley had always lived alone. Ten minutes after showing Billy where everything was, he was already jumpy.

Billy tossed his bag onto the couch in the den. "I'm going to see Veronica," he said.

"There's an extra key in the drawer," Farley said.

Veronica's tía stood in the doorway, arms crossed, not saying anything to Billy, but her expression told him everything he needed to know.

"Is Veronica here?" he asked.

In reply, she turned, closing the door behind her. Billy was debating whether to knock again when the door opened and Veronica stepped outside.

She touched his cheek, and he flinched. "What happened to your face?"

Billy looked down. "My dad kicked me out. I'm staying at Farley's for the time being."

"My tía says she's not raising another baby."

"I could sell the Barracuda," Billy said. It was the most valuable thing he owned.

"But you love your car."

Billy shrugged. "It's just a car."

Veronica's smile was tinged with sadness. "I can't let you do that."

Billy kicked the dirt. Even if he got a job tomorrow, it wasn't like they'd advance him a month's salary. He needed money and needed it soon.

"I could race it for pink slips on Forest Lane."

"What do you mean?"

"I own it free and clear. I could put the title up against another car's. If I win, I'd get the other guy's car and turn around and sell it."

"And if you lose?"

"I won't lose." Having never raced, Billy spoke with a conviction he didn't feel.

"How do you know you can find someone to race?"

"I rebuilt a Holley four-barrel for a guy who heard I was good with cars. Skip Parker. Shorted me ten dollars on the job, said that I charged more than the work was worth. He likes to brag about how fast his Mustang is, but I know that car better than he does."

"Why would you even trust him?"

Billy shrugged. "We'd find someone to hold the titles while we race."

"Your car's nice and all, but is it really fast?"

"Not like the muscle cars that came out after, but she'll beat Skip's Mustang, even with the rebuilt carb."

Veronica's expression seemed to veer between hope and despair. But all Billy could see was the cash Skip's Mustang represented, money he'd use to rent him and Veronica their own place. Billy imagined fanning the bills in his hand, inhaling their smell, his future a road running straight and true.

2021

Twilight fell. Billy stood by the window, trying to still his mind. He wondered if it was force of habit that had kept him here all these years. The house never was worth much, but selling it would have given him a stake, surely enough to start over someplace new. He remembered talking with Farley shortly before he died, Billy saying how if he could go back in time, he'd do things differently.

"You'd just make different mistakes," Farley had said. "You're a good man who ran into some bad luck. Just like your father, that way."

Billy didn't bother arguing their differences because ultimately, there was no doubt he was Ernest Wright's son. To be sure, Billy had been less prejudiced, and he'd truly loved a girl, but he'd made no more of himself than his father had. Billy couldn't say why. If he hadn't gotten Veronica pregnant, he suspected something else would have gotten in his way.

What he was planning now was just a shot in the dark. But at sixty-two, he was on the downslope of his life, and part of him thought all this had to be coming together for a reason.

He laughed at how he sounded like the radio televangelists he listened to sometimes when he was driving late at night, their disembodied voices with their earnest rhythms oddly calming. Not that Billy had ever believed, but you didn't have to be a Christian to understand the lessons they tried to impart. And what would they say about him now?

Billy pocketed his phone and headed to Huey's back lot, following the detour he'd taken earlier. As he neared the lot, Billy killed the Jeep's lights and backed into a loading dock, parking in front of a dumpster.

The night air was alive with sounds. Insects he couldn't see hummed and whirred like something mechanical. Cutting through that was the grinding chatter of an impact wrench, followed by the chunk and rumble of an air compressor kicking on.

When Billy's eyes adjusted to the dark, he crept forward, keeping to the shadows. A pair of portable spotlights on Huey's lot glowed like something alive. Using just his arms, Billy pulled himself up the fence to get a better view. Two men stood by the Barracuda's open passenger-side door. Something jostled one of the lights, its beam like a flare in the night. He shrank back, hoping no one saw him. As soon as the spotlight steadied, Billy dropped to the ground and went back to the Jeep.

He rubbed the cuts of the Barracuda's key to bring him luck. At midnight, the spotlights cut off. A few minutes later, the gate opened, and a single vehicle exited, heading away from him. Once it was out of sight, Billy tossed a blanket over his right shoulder. He climbed the fence a second time, his motions smooth, the fence quiet. When he was eye level with the top, he tucked his boots into the fence and listened.

Whistling, faint and in tune, but unnerving. Something from a movie. Then it hit him—that crazy theme from *The Good, the Bad and the Ugly*. For a long moment, Billy perched on the fence, feeling like a moth on a screen door. But soon the whistling faded, and Billy knew he had to make his move.

He spread the folded blanket over the barbed wire and tested his grip. Some of the barbs poked through, and he positioned his hands between them, before swinging his right leg over. His shirt snagged on one of the barbs. Billy pulled it free, ignoring the dots of blood blossoming in the fabric. He swung his other leg over the blanket, doing his best to keep his jeans above the wire.

At the edge of his vision, headlights cut the darkness. Billy tugged on the blanket, trying to free it. Finally, he snaked his hand underneath and pushed the blanket over his head, letting it drop behind him. He scrambled down the fence, flattening himself on the ground. The headlight wash stopped just short of where he lay. He recognized the car as the one that had left earlier, which set his heart to pounding even harder.

The car idled at the gate, and Billy heard a miss in the engine. The shoemaker's son always goes barefoot, he figured. The horn honked twice, some signal between the driver and the whistler, Billy thought, before it continued down the alley.

He crouched as he walked along the fence line, freezing when his boots crunched against some gravel. Hearing nothing from the garage, Billy continued. When a door opened, he squatted behind a stack of tires, peering through a narrow gap between them at the Barracuda, parked directly across from him. Even as he worried about whoever was on the other side of that door,

Billy couldn't help but admire the lines and curves of the car, its still-gleaming paint lit by an LED looming above the lot like a cyclops.

"You just made the worst mistake of your life." The male voice cut through the night, locking Billy in place. The footsteps grew closer as the man paused on the far side of the Barracuda. The zigzag scar on his cheek looked wet under the light. When he rounded the car, Billy saw that he held a double-barrel shotgun. The man racked the slide.

Billy's bowels loosened, and he held his breath, idly wondering if there was any way he could talk himself out of being shot. The man wore a blue uniform like Tish's, except there was no patch with his name on it. His lips formed a sneer, as if he were in on a joke Billy was outside of. He took another step toward Billy.

Billy felt the air shift, and the man wheeled like a drum major, marching for the corner of the lot where the blanket lay. When he picked it up, Billy moved in a low arc toward the car and squatted behind the Barracuda's trunk, hoping the man thought Billy had climbed over the fence, gone back the way he'd come. The man's voice sounded, his words indistinct, his footsteps like a hammer's tapping. Billy knew he had one chance to get this right or his last sight would be the business end of the shotgun.

He fitted the key to the lock and turned it as slowly and silently as he could, until the trunk opened with a dull pop. Billy slipped inside, keeping the lid close to his shoulder. He pulled it down, not latching it until that infernal whistling pierced the night again.

He'd gotten lucky. The security panel was up, so no one could see him from the outside. Billy lay in the fetal position, the air around him already stale, the rough carpet pressed against his cheek familiar.

His body jerked in surprise when the man tried the door handles one by one. At the trunk, Billy heard the man's fingers slip into the gap between the trunk lid and the car's body. The car rose, and Billy felt as if he were floating in embryonic darkness.

When the footsteps finally receded from his hearing, Billy allowed himself to exhale, understanding that this had been the easy part.

1976

"Concentrate on your tach," Farley said. "Make your shifts before redline so your wheels don't spin."

Billy nodded. Farley didn't work on his own truck, but he knew how to drive. According to Billy's father, he'd raced on dirt tracks when he was younger.

"I can go with you, if you want," Farley said.

"No need," Billy said. "One of the football players is going to hold the pink slips, and two brothers who've been unofficially running some races will be at the start and finish."

Farley nodded, but Billy didn't think he was convinced. The truth was, this was Billy's mess, and he was determined to fix it himself. He told Veronica he'd call her the next morning. The race wasn't until late, and she said there was no way her tía would let her go. Having Skip see her in his corner would have been sweet, but Billy knew he had to stay focused. Besides, he and Veronica had spent so much time together in his car, he always felt as if she were right next to him in the passenger seat.

As Billy cruised down Forest Lane, the crowds reminded him of those on the Fourth of July. Cars were backed up onto the street at the Jack in the Box drive-thru, and every car Billy saw was full of kids, front seat and back. Billy's own car hardly stood out among the newer muscle cars, particularly a red '70 Hemi 'Cuda with hockey stick stripes that caught his eye. That car would blow the doors off his Barracuda, but the only car he had to beat tonight was Skip's Mustang 2+2. On paper, it was a tick faster in the quarter mile, having more horsepower and a bigger engine, as well as being lighter. But after Billy rebuilt the Mustang's carb, he rode with Skip when he test-drove it. He saw that Skip liked to ride the clutch, which Billy could tell was starting to slip. The Barracuda's clutch was tight as a drum, and the Hurst shifter felt like an extension of his hand. He thought that would be worth a few tenths of a second over the course of the quarter-mile race.

Billy pulled into Chief Auto where he'd agreed to meet Skip. Their race would start about a mile away, at the psychedelic mural the W.T. White kids had recently painted on the wall separating the neighborhood on the north side of Forest Lane from the road.

When Billy got out of the Barracuda, Skip sauntered toward him, trailed by three guys and a handful of girls. Skip had feathered blond hair and tight Levi's, and he wore driving loafers and leather gloves with holes in the knuckles. Billy had on his lucky Mopar T-shirt, jeans, and boots, the only clothes he was ever comfortable in.

"Billy Wright," Skip started. "I didn't think you had the balls to ever race this pig. What changed your mind?"

Billy crossed his arms. "Got tired of all your yapping about how fast your Mustang is."

Skip's eyes bore into Billy's. "You'll see soon enough."

Checking out the course, Billy drove slowly down the right lane, looking for anything that could slow the Barracuda, but the surface was clean and smooth. Back at the start, he focused on the road ahead. Mike Hall, who everyone said had a chance to be the next Bob Lilly, held the pink slips. The Barrett brothers stood at the start and at the big end of the quarter mile, which was marked by a traffic cone on the centerline. On Billy's left, Skip raced the Mustang's engine.

Billy ran his damp palms through his hair and took a few deep breaths, telling himself not to think of all he could lose, but of what winning the race meant—a home for Veronica and him and the baby to come. Nothing else mattered.

Sixteen seconds, three shifts, four hundred forty yards.

Ed Barrett raised his right hand. Billy revved the Barracuda's engine to 4,000 RPM, the tach dancing tiny steps back and forth. Ed dropped his hand, and Billy slipped the clutch until the tires caught, surging off the line without wheelspin. The Barracuda jumped ahead of the Mustang. Holeshot, Billy thought.

He kept the pedal to the floor and listened as, behind him, the Mustang's engine ran at a higher pitch and was getting louder.

Just before the tach reached 6,000 RPM, Billy jabbed the clutch and shifted into second. To his right, the mural was a blur. To his left, Skip had begun gaining back the ground he'd lost at the start.

For the first time, doubt flickered in Billy's mind. He forced it down, even when Skip's car pulled ahead—bumper, fender, and door handle—his lead steadily widening.

Billy concentrated on keeping the Barracuda as straight as possible, one eye on the tach, which had begun its clockwise dance again, the engine roaring as it passed 6,000 RPM. He shifted into third, the motions of his hands and feet automatic. Ahead, Tom Barrett stood on the shoulder at the big end.

The instant some dissonance in the Mustang's drivetrain struck Billy's ear, he knew he was going to win. The Barracuda came momentarily even with Skip's car and kept going, its front wheels ahead of the Mustang's bumper now, the speedometer kissing eighty. He was filled with love for Veronica, as their life together began to take new form in his head.

Billy glanced in the side-view mirror as a flash of iridescent spray crossed his field of view. His world went silent. The Barracuda's tires somehow lost grip, and Skip passed the traffic cone half a car length ahead of Billy.

He pulled over and felt numb, until he pieced together what Skip had done. Red with anger now, and seeing all his plans in pieces, Billy stomped toward a smirking Skip.

"Tough break, Billy boy," he said.

"You son of a bitch," Billy said. He slammed his palms into Skip's chest. "You cheated."

He pushed past Skip, but before he could get near the Mustang, arms closed around him. Skip's friends.

Now Skip stood in front of him. "What did you say to me?"

Billy struggled against the guys who held him. "You heard me. You sprayed something on the road—I saw it in the side mirror when I passed you."

"You didn't see shit."

Billy pulled one arm free. "Prove it."

Skip turned to the Mustang. "You want to look?"

Too late Billy saw Skip's fist swinging forward. He slipped the punch, but the following uppercut to his gut doubled him over. The guys behind him shoved him to the ground and began kicking him. Billy covered his head, but their boots found his ribs.

Billy pushed himself up and lunged for Skip's loafers, figuring if he was going to take a pounding, he'd at least make sure he got one good punch in. Someone hit him from behind. The blow scrambled his thoughts, for the last thing he saw was Veronica, floating beyond his reach, receding into a void that felt like emptiness.

2021

Voices woke Billy. His body knotted and cramped, he found himself in a darkness so complete it was as if he were no longer of this earth, until memory oriented him. Billy fished in his pocket for his phone and realized with horror he hadn't put it in silent mode. It was after seven, and Huey's lot was coming to life. Billy figured the men working on the Barracuda last night were getting it ready for transport today. He didn't have much time.

Much as it pained him to do so, he drove his elbow into the security panel separating the trunk from the area behind the seats until he'd punched it free. Gray light filled the interior, and he climbed over the rear seat. Crouching below window level, he slowly raised his head until he could see the lot. No one was to the left or right of him, but ahead, one of Huey's men stood by the automatic gate as a flatbed approached.

No point in waiting, Billy thought. He slipped between the front seats and slid behind the steering wheel. The wood was smooth and burnished, and he felt transported to the past, the years slipping away in an instant. He turned to his right, as if expecting to see teenage Veronica in the passenger seat.

The sound of the gate opening focused his mind. He slumped behind the wheel as one of the men pointed at the Barracuda. Instead of running toward him, the man turned to the flatbed's driver. The truck's diesel began clattering, its backup warning ringing steadily. Huey's man glanced at the Barracuda a second time, before waving the truck on.

Billy started the engine, the Barracuda's low rumble embracing him like a long-lost friend. The tach dancing as he gave the engine gas, Billy remembered how it sounded at redline, two hundred thirty-five horsepower making the engine feel like something alive. He rolled down the window and put his arm on the sill, the metal warm. Nothing's changed, he thought, and shifted into first.

The expression on Huey's man's face swung between surprise and confusion. Billy waved to reassure him. When the automatic gate started to close, his plan for a nonchalant exit vanished. He stomped on the gas, and the Barracuda caught rubber, the car fishtailing as it headed straight for the flatbed. He waited until he was less than a car length away to swerve around it. The automatic gate was still open wide enough for the Barracuda to get through, but a truck towing a double-wide trailer took up the entire width of the alley to Billy's left, where, because of the angle he was taking around the flatbed, he'd have to exit. Billy leaned on the horn as he cleared the lot. One of Huey's men dove to the right as the gate kissed the rear bumper. Billy slammed on the brakes, and the Barracuda skidded to a stop just short of the truck. The driver glared at him and revved the truck's engine. Billy ignored him and turned to his left. Huey stood beside the flatbed, arms crossed, expression unreadable. In a suit, he looked incongruous among the men in work clothes who scrambled toward the fence.

Huey made a pistol out of his right hand and fired it at Billy. Billy nodded. He shifted into reverse, planning a move that was straightforward in its execution, requiring only a forty-five-year-old muscle memory.

He accelerated backwards, and once he'd reached the end of Huey's lot, flicked the steering wheel to the left. The car spun to the right as if on ice, and Billy found himself one-hundred eighty degrees from where he started, the tow truck small in the rear-view mirror. He shifted into first and punched the accelerator.

Once out of the industrial park, Billy swung onto Harry Hines, needing to put some distance between him and Huey's. As he changed lanes, Billy constantly checked his mirrors to make sure he wasn't being followed. He was aware of how much the Barracuda stood out in a sea of uniformly bland SUVs and pickups, which he knew was going to be a problem.

He was thinking it would be smart to find a parking garage when his phone buzzed. Billy figured it was Huey, delivering bad news. Not having mastered the art of driving and using the phone simultaneously, Billy took the next exit and drove a few blocks until he found street parking. A notification on his phone read, "AirTag found moving with you. The location of this AirTag can be seen by the owner." Billy didn't know what an AirTag was. A quick search on his phone showed a picture of the tracker, which was small enough to hide anywhere. Billy needed a place to work. He saw a sign for hospital parking and entered a garage. He drove to the lowest level, where he had no signal and few cars were parked, and backed into a spot.

Billy closed his eyes and inhaled deeply, trying to slow his racing heart. Last night the men had been working on the right side of the car. Billy walked to the passenger side and opened the door, looking for anything that seemed off. He removed the floor mat and felt the carpet and under the seat. Nothing. The glove compartment held only the title, signed by Skip, and the original owner's manual, the pages still bearing Billy's greasy thumb-prints, faded now.

He didn't have much time. If Huey's men followed his track to where it ended, they would start searching the garage and watching the exits. Billy leaned against the car, his hand on the door. At the bottom, one corner of the panel wasn't fully seated. He squatted and worked his fingers underneath, popping the panel from the door along the bottom and up each side. He ran his fingers inside the well and found a leather keyring holding a steel disk engraved with an apple.

Billy couldn't figure out why Huey needed to track a car being delivered by a flatbed he'd arranged for. It made no sense. He felt under the door again, this time reaching up with both hands. His fingers hit plastic, and Billy's first thought was drugs. He tore the package free and found himself looking at bundles of cash shrink-wrapped together.

He shoved the cash under the front seat and slapped the panel back into place. When a pickup drove past, Billy tossed the AirTag keyring into the truck's bed without breaking stride. Worried he could somehow be tracked by his phone too, Billy ground the screen under his boot heel and dumped the pieces in separate trash bins.

During the ten minutes he waited—long enough for Huey's men to follow the tracker but not so long that they'd double back to the garage—Billy weighed his options. Because she'd kept her last name, he assumed Veronica was single now, and he figured, as far as her place from civilization was, she lived alone. If he was wrong about that, then he guessed his visit was going to be a short one. Indulging his hope, he told himself if she'd been single all this time, maybe a part of her still loved him. Billy figured Huey's reach didn't extend into Mexico. The cash meant he and Veronica could drive away from their old lives and start anew together.

Taking state roads, Billy worked his way northwest toward her place. He needed to get the Barracuda out of sight. Following a sign for lodging, he found a Super 8 near Denton and parked around back, where the Barracuda was at least hidden from the main road. He put on a mask, glad for once to be wearing it, since he figured Huey would be broadcasting his description, along with the car's, up and down the interstates. The clerk told him he could do an early check-in at noon.

He drove to a Target near Texas Woman's University and bought some toiletries and snacks. He'd been wearing the same clothes for two days and knew he was overdue for a change. He picked up what he needed, along with a backpack. Back in his car, he reached under the passenger seat and put the shrink-wrapped cash in the backpack, covering it with the rest of his purchases.

Billy had an hour and a half to kill, and he had to get off the street, where he felt his car did nothing but stand out. A United Methodist Church looked promising, until he saw the empty parking lot. Past the church, on the right, was the entrance for South Lakes Park. He followed the main road until he came to a parking lot, which was half full. Billy figured this was as good as it was going to get. He backed into a spot and got out of the car, his backpack looped over one shoulder. A copse of trees in sight of the lot offered the possibility of shade and, he hoped, the ability to see anyone coming before they saw him.

No one came.

Back at the motel, he showered and shaved and put on his new blue Dickies and black T-shirt. With the curtains closed and the air conditioning cranked, the motel room was an oasis of cool. Billy hefted the shrink-wrapped cash before cutting the plastic free. The tower of bundles toppled. He riffled one to check the denominations. All hundreds. The other bundles were the same. Until today, Veronica had been the biggest break he'd gotten in his life, and that barely lasted a summer. Now he had to convince her that this cash was a second chance for them both.

What Billy thought was going to be one last joyride had just turned into something else.

1976

Billy felt the car slow. Someone pulled him upright and reached across his chest for the door handle. Then he was propelled sideways, falling into the gutter. The car sped off, its rear tires spitting gravel that stung his face. He tried to push himself up, but the stabbing in his sides forced him back down. Blood dripped from his nose, spotting the asphalt like rust. He rolled onto his back, the few stars above as formless as lint.

Everything hurt, but the pain was only a backdrop to the finality of losing his car. All the love he'd put into it, that was gone now, along with whatever chance he had to make a future with Veronica and the baby to come.

He coughed up phlegm, and the pain was searing. Groaning, he managed to make it onto his knees. A car drove by, and the passenger threw a bottle at him. Billy ducked, but the bottle caught the back of his head, the sound of laughter the last thing he heard before the world went black for a second time that night.

He woke in his father's arms. After carrying him into their house and lowering him to the couch, his father left without saying anything. Billy guessed there'd been nothing to say. He heard water running and turned his head. His father carried a steel basin and put it on the coffee table. He dipped a washcloth into the basin and daubed the blood from Billy's face. Each time he wrung it out, the water went crimson and brown, dirt and blood mixing, turning the water ocher.

When he was done, he handed Billy two cotton balls. "Stick these up your nose."

Billy felt the swelling on his face and figured he must look bad.

"Do you want to tell me what happened?"

Billy looked away, trying to put words to the night. Now that he had nothing, he knew he had nothing to lose with the unvarnished truth.

"I raced Skip Parker for pink slips," he started, recalling every detail of the race. "I knew the Barracuda was faster and figured after I won, I'd sell his car so that me and Veronica could get a place of our own. I was passing Skip's Mustang when the Barracuda lost traction. He rigged his car to spray something—probably transmission fluid—onto the road. I accused him of cheating, and he and his friends kicked my ass and dumped me out front."

His father didn't seem angry, and it didn't look like he thought Billy was a fool.

"How bad are you hurt?" he asked.

Billy pushed himself up, wincing. "It's mostly my ribs. The sting like hell whenever I move."

"They're probably broken. Not much you can do except wait for them to heal. If you start coughing up blood, we'll have to take you to the hospital."

"No hospital," Billy said.

"Can you see all right?"

Billy nodded.

"Your nose is going to be a little crooked from now on, but nothing that will scare the girls off."

Billy couldn't image being with any girl but Veronica, and he was afraid that was going to be over soon anyway.

"How come you're not mad at me?" he asked.

"What good would that do?" Now his father looked off. "Besides, I know you did what you thought you had to because I didn't give you much choice."

His father stood and carried the basin into the bathroom and returned with two pills and a glass of water. "For the pain," he said, handing them to Billy.

"What are they?" he asked, before swallowing them.

"Codeine. Left over from when I busted up my hand fishing."

Billy remembered how the bandage on his father's left hand

looked like a boxing glove. He drank some more of the water.

"Does Skip have the title?"

"Title and car both."

His father nodded. "You're sure he cheated?"

Billy hesitated. "I *know* the car lost grip. Had my eye on the side-view mirror when I was passing Skip, and something came off his car. Afterwards, he wouldn't let me get near it."

Billy knew how weak it sounded, but he also knew his car.

"Did you bring anyone with you?"

"I didn't think I needed to." Billy didn't have a lot of friends, certainly no one who'd stand with him when it came time to throw hands.

His father stood. "Try to sleep. If your pain gets bad, the pills are right there. Don't take too many."

The lights went out, and Billy pulled the old afghan over top of him. He shook a handful of pills into his palm and washed them down with what was left of the water. Soon the pain receded, and he was left with only a dull ache that left him feeling detached from all that had happened. He reran the race in his head, hearing the V8 respond with each shift, seeing Skip's Mustang recede in his mirror as the Barracuda's headlights carved windows into the endless darkness.

Billy woke in the afternoon, his mouth dry, his memory fuzzy. His face in the bathroom mirror was mottled with bruises, the cotton in his nostrils black with dried blood. While he was splashing cold water onto his face, he thought he heard the phone ring and his father's voice. When he emerged from the bathroom, his father stood in the kitchen.

"You don't look too bad."

"Liar," he said.

His father laughed. "You got me there."

Billy nodded at the phone. "Who called?"

"Wrong number."

Billy nodded. He noticed that the pill bottle was gone, not that it mattered. For a few hours, he'd been able to forget everything that happened. Billy knew he should talk to Veronica, but he didn't know what he'd say to her.

When his father went out to pick up some carry-out, Billy called Farley and told him what happened.

"I was there," Farley started.

"What?" Billy said. "There was no need—you'd already done enough, letting me stay with you."

"Your girl snuck out of her house and knocked on my door after midnight. I thought it was the cops. She asked me to take her to Forest Lane."

"Did you see the race?"

The line was quiet for a beat before Farley spoke. "We got there right as you started but couldn't get too close. It looked like your car was running good until near the end. Before we could check on you, someone said the cops were on their way. Veronica wanted to see you, but I told her we needed to get her out of there."

"You did the right thing," Billy said, relieved Veronica didn't witness him getting the shit kicked out of him by Skip and his buddies. "Skip cheated. He rigged up his car to spray something slick on the road. There's no way I can prove it now, but I know what I saw. They put a hurtin' on me when I complained."

"I'm sorry about what happened. I know how much you loved that car."

And Veronica, Billy thought. "Well, I'd better go."

"Take care now, Billy."

It took Billy two days to work up the nerve to call Veronica. He figured she knew he'd lost the race, and he had no idea what to tell her.

"She's not here, Billy," her tía said. "She lost the baby and is staying with her cousin in El Paso."

"Can I have the number there?"

"Look, Billy. You're a nice kid, but you're not right for Veronica. Do you know what I'm saying? It's better for her if you don't see her again."

"No, I—"

"I'm sorry. Please don't call again."

Billy looked at the phone. He told himself somehow he'd find Veronica and get his car back and make right everything that had gone wrong.

2021

Billy waited until twilight to head west. Wanting to avoid the interstate, he worked his way through the neighborhoods bracketing the highway. For a while, it was slow going, but it gave Billy time to rehearse what he'd say to Veronica. He considered worst case scenarios, all of which involved an imposing husband and extended family living with her. If that proved to be the case, he'd ask for a moment of her time and make his pitch. But in his heart of hearts, he knew she was living alone, and had been for a long time.

By the time he cleared Denton and was on the farm-to-market road headed to Krum, it was full dark. Low-rise, brick-front buildings marked the downtown. A few blocks later the buildings were gone, replaced by single-family houses, until he cleared what he supposed were the town's limits. Now farmland, bordered by scrub trees and wire fencing, flanked the road.

Billy didn't know what to make of all that open space. Where he lived, sounds from the neighbors and traffic never faded, a kind of white noise that had become so familiar he no longer heard it. With the car window down, he heard only the rumble of the tires and the rush of the wind. Veronica had grown up near him. He wondered how she'd adjusted to the change and how long it had taken her.

At one point, Billy killed the lights and let the Barracuda drift onto the shoulder. Craning his head beyond the door jamb, he looked up to a night sky bright with stars in constellations he couldn't name.

He kept driving.

When he finally reached Veronica's place, it had been twenty minutes since he'd last seen a car, longer since he'd seen a person outside. The last thing he wanted to do after forty-five years was bring trouble to her. He took one final look into his mirrors at the empty road behind him and turned onto her gravel driveway.

Halfway down was a minivan, and he worried that all his assumptions about her were wrong. He inched the Barracuda around it, parking where his car was mostly shielded from view. He killed the engine and in the ensuing silence heard only his breath, coming faster now as his heart pounded like a tappet.

Clock's ticking, he told himself.

He got out of the car and cupped his hands to the minivan's window, peering inside. He noticed the van's door was unlocked, something he couldn't imagine ever doing back home. A teddy bear with a red bow under its chin sat on the passenger seat. A grandchild's, he guessed, his heart sinking. He walked to the front of the house and stood under an awning, backpack slung over one shoulder. A door knocker in the shape of an iguana peered back him. Before he could change his mind, he grabbed its head and gave the door three good raps.

The door opened, bound by the security chain. Veronica's face filled the gap, and he felt the wonder he had when he saw her for the first time.

"Billy, is that really you?" Her voice was friendly, as if she were greeting someone she didn't quite remember.

He wiped the sweat from his forehead with the back of his hand. "It's great to see you."

"What brings you out here?"

"It's kind of a long story. I was hoping we could talk."

"I'm sorry. Won't you come in?"

This time he heard warmth in her voice, and his shoulders relaxed. She closed the door and released the chain before leading him inside to a living room with wide-planked floors and simple wooden furniture topped by thick cushions. A fireplace against one wall was swept clean. Above it was a poster of a Frida Kahlo painting.

He pointed. "I still have the postcard you gave me."

Veronica's expression faltered. "That was a long time ago."

She motioned him to one of the chairs, and he sat. Despite the heat, she wore jeans and a flannel shirt, plain clothes that didn't flatter her. Her only concessions to fashion were turquoise boots, which brought Billy back to the Fourth of July and all that happened after.

"Would you like something to drink?"

"Do you have Mexican Coke?"

"Of course." Veronica went through an open doorway into a small kitchen, and Billy looked around the living room. It held the clutter of a person who lived alone—magazines piled on an ottoman, a small desk covered with papers—but wasn't impersonal, filled as it was with a shelf full of art books and framed posters on all the walls. Billy liked how the colors made the place feel warm and homey.

Veronica handed him a glass and sat with her own on the adjacent loveseat. Her face was fuller and her cheeks rounder, but her eyes shone with brightness and her smile was genuine. At some point while they were talking, the image Billy held in his head of her teenage self was finally replaced by the here-and-now version of Veronica, forty-five years compressed and accelerated to this moment.

"I like your place," he said. "But what brought you all the way out here?"

"I work in the city, and I wanted to come home to something completely different. No crowds or traffic. It's so quiet there's times I swear I can hear the stars wheel overhead. What about you?"

"I'm still in Old East Dallas in Dad's house."

She tilted her head. "Is he still alive?"

"He had a stroke not long after—after the race. I found him on his bedroom floor. At first, I thought he'd passed out drunk. When I finally went to wake him, he was stiff as a board."

"Oh, Billy. That's awful. I'm so sorry."

"It's funny. He took care of me when I got beat up after the race, and we'd finally started really talking."

Veronica raised her eyebrows. "When I didn't hear from you that morning, I called you in the afternoon. Your dad said you didn't want to speak to me. He told me I'd cost you everything and should never call back. I wanted to hear it from you, but things happened so fast after."

Billy felt the room sway. He leaned forward, elbows on his knees, his face in his hands.

"Billy, are you all right?"

He moaned, his anger against his father erupting all over again. "Dad never said you called. When *I* called *you*, your tía told me you lost the baby and were staying with a cousin. She wouldn't give me her number."

Veronica faced him. "I didn't lose the baby, Billy. I had an abortion and stayed with my cousin after."

Billy didn't know what to say. He knew he was in no position to judge her now, and back then, he'd been in no position to help.

She looked down. "I wasn't ready to raise a child on my own and—and I thought you didn't want anything more to do with me."

He shook his head, feeling the hurt all over again. "None of this should have happened. Skip cheated in the race, my dad lied to you—"

"Billy, stop. Please. You can't undo any of it."

But I can, Billy thought. He shifted the backpack's strap against his shoulder. Before he could speak, Veronica's brow wrinkled.

"How did you find me?"

"I remembered how much you liked Frida and did a search with your name and hers. Your blog said you lived in Krum, so I checked the property tax records and got your address."

Veronica glanced at the poster. "I haven't thought about that blog in years."

Billy nodded at the door. "I saw your minivan. Do you have kids?"

Veronica smiled. "No kids. Clients. I'm an immigration attorney, and sometimes I have to bring entire families to court."

"A lawyer. Does that pay well?"

"Most of my clients don't have much money, or they have debts. It's so hard for them. I work with an organization that tries to help." She crossed her legs. "The last four years have been difficult."

"It sounds like you do good work."

"We try," she said.

Billy debated his next words, but having come this far and risked so much, there wasn't much question. "I never stopped loving you, Veronica."

"Don't say that."

"It's true."

"Don't *say* that. You don't love me—you love the memory of what we had. That was a long time ago."

"Forty-five years."

"People change."

Billy blinked back tears. "I haven't."

"Maybe that's the problem. Look, I cared for you then, but it was never going to work. Your dad, my tía. We had no money, no prospects. After you lost the car—I'm sorry, but I did what I had to so that I could make something of myself. And when your dad said I'd ruined your life and that you didn't want to see me again, I knew that lie was easier to live with than the truth. Part of me hoped I'd see you again, but another part knew it was better if I didn't."

Billy felt worse than when Veronica disappeared because there'd always been the possibility he'd find her again. And now he had. Billy didn't bother wiping the tears that ran down his cheeks.

He got up. "There's something I need to show you."

45

Veronica tilted her head.

"Please." He held out his hand.

She stood without taking it. Once they were outside, he gestured toward the Barracuda, waiting for her reaction.

Veronica brought both hands to her face. "Oh, Billy. Your car—it looks so nice. How did you get it back?"

Billy ran his hand along the Barracuda's roofline. "It still drives like a dream. All these years, it's just like I remembered." He opened the driver's side door. "Pretty as it ever was." He glanced over his shoulder. "Just like you."

When Veronica didn't come any nearer, Billy looked away. Maybe a half mile down the road stood another house, formless except for a milky glow from its windows. Behind Veronica's place the land ran flat to a line of trees like fringe on the horizon. Next to the road, telephone poles marched as far as he could see, their convergence lost in the darkness.

"Would you be willing to walk away from it all—your home, everyone you know—for a second chance with me?"

"What are you talking about?"

"I saw my car at Huey's Auto yesterday and took it back this morning. While I was getting rid of the tracker they stuck inside the door, I found this cash." He lifted the backpack. "There's enough money in here for us to start over anywhere we want. I was thinking Mexico."

"Billy, are you crazy? I can't believe you did this—what if someone followed you here? That car is like a ticking time bomb. You need to leave now."

Whatever warmth and concern there'd been in her voice earlier was gone. Billy understood his hope of a second chance with Veronica had always been a pipe dream.

He looped the backpack over his shoulder. "If anyone asks, you don't know anything about any money. I just came by to see you on my way out of town."

Billy leaned in to kiss her, but she shoved both hands into his chest.

"Just go, Billy. Now."

A car drove by without slowing. Billy watched until its tail-lights faded like tracers. By the time it was out of sight, Veronica had gone inside. He looked over his shoulder before opening the door to her minivan. The center console held some old-school AAA road maps and a Spanish-language Bible. Billy didn't believe in miracles and doubted Veronica did either but figured he could at least help a little. Where he was going, he wouldn't need all the money anyway.

He lined the bottom of the console with bundles of cash and covered them with the maps and Bible. Leaving a single penny on top of the console as a clue for her to look inside, he locked the van door before shutting it.

The Barracuda's engine rumbled to life. He backed out of the driveway and onto the road. Revving the engine as punctuation before shifting into first, he recognized that the past was finally behind him now.

The miles ticked by, and Billy told himself no one was follow-ing him. The road ran pancake flat, straight and true, and the few houses he saw looked buttoned up for the night. He kept an eye on the rear-view mirror. At some point, headlights from a car behind him sliced the darkness like daggers. He sped up, and the trailing car accelerated with him. The Barracuda could still move, but whatever Huey's man was driving was bound to have more horsepower and better handling. He figured someone had seen his car, and word got back to Huey. For the second time in his life, what he thought of as a way out was turning into just another dead end.

The remaining cash was in his backpack on the passenger seat. Billy unzipped it with his right hand, the bundles inside slick to his touch, their smell acrid. He hoped this money was Skip's. Billy didn't have any idea what Skip was buying with the cash and the Barracuda, which he figured was part of the deal, but that transaction was null and void now.

The car behind him flashed its high beams, signaling Billy to pull over. If he did, the driver would politely ask him for the money and his keys before putting two bullets in the back of his head.

"I don't play that," he said.

He grabbed one of the bundles and tore the wrapper. Holding the cash out the window, he thought the bills sounded like cards being shuffled. He flicked his wrist, and the cash got caught in the Barracuda's slipstream, a green tail fluttering behind him.

The chasing car slowed, and Billy understood the driver's dilemma—should he stop for the cash, which, along with the car, he was expected to recover, or should he continue in pursuit of Billy?

The car sped forward, horn honking now, and Billy had his answer. He tugged the backpack onto his lap and, the steering wheel held between his knees, began tearing the wrappers as fast as he could. He'd seen a movie once where wind swirled autumn leaves in a miniature cyclone. As he flung the bundles from the car, he remembered that he hadn't liked the ending of that movie. He knew the one he was acting in now would turn out no better.

The car was right on his bumper, and Billy tossed the empty backpack out the window. It stuck to the pursuing car's windshield, and the car swerved off the road, contrails of dust spiraling behind it.

Ahead, he saw a shimmer of metal, and he slowed and flipped on his high beams. Two cars, nose to tail at an obtuse angle, blocked the road. Beside them were two men armed with shotguns.

So, this is where it ends, Billy thought. In the rear-view mirror, the car that had gone onto the shoulder was behind him again, but farther back. He guessed the driver knew there was no hurry now.

Billy let the car coast, watching as the men took a step forward, their weapons held at their waists. He depressed the clutch and revved the engine. Both men raised their guns, and Billy waved, as if to say, "Just kidding."

Instead, thinking the two men should have brought long guns if they really wanted to stop him, he gave the Barracuda more gas until the tach was at redline.

He popped the clutch, and the Barracuda shot forward, rear tires chirping. The shotgun barrels flamed as Billy upshifted, the tach climbing again, the engine roaring as God intended it to.

The two men ran behind their cars, shotgun stocks against their shoulders, four barrels pointed at Billy. Aiming dead center and hoping for a split, he pressed the pedal to the floor. The Barracuda found even more speed.

Billy closed his eyes. The windshield shattered, the subsequent wash of wind and glass peppering his head and shoulders until something heavier rent his body. He no longer heard the Barracuda's engine.

Through his closed eyes, flames filled Billy's vision. He passed above this earth, imagining Veronica's arms around him now, the smoldering wreckage of the Barracuda below him a silent memorial to his love.

DEVIL IN THE REARVIEW

Stephen D. Rogers

Liza waited until the pickup truck reached the end of the driveway before climbing up into the cab. Leaning out of the vehicle, she grabbed hold of the door, and closed it as quietly as two-hundred pounds of swinging metal could be stopped.

Crossing her fingers, she started the engine. So loud!

The rumble became a roar as she pressed the accelerator.

Please let none of those sounds be loud enough to wake Gary.

Liza sped down the dark street and took the next right.

How many times should she have to put up with being hit until she stole his baby? Turned out the answer was one less than yesterday.

She snapped on the high beams and called Oscar.

Ringing, ringing, ringing.

"Ahoy!" Apparently, woken from a dream.

"Remember that guy you knew?" She glanced in the rearview before taking the next left. Still no sign of Gary.

"How about a hello?"

"Hello, Oscar. Remember that guy you knew?"

"Sweetie, I've known so many guys it would make your head spin."

"The car guy."

"You got to narrow it down, Liza Lee. Front seat? Back seat? Hood? There was that one time in a trunk."

"Oscar, focus, I'm racing the clock here. The guy who buys cars. On the side." She took the next right.

"You mean Huey?"

"Yeah, Huey, if Huey's his name. How many guys you know chop stolen vehicles, Oscar?"

"Just the one."

"Then I'm betting that's him."

Oscar laughed. "Yes, Liza, I still know Huey. Just saw him at a party last week. Don't want to hurt his feelings, but I think his hairline might be receding."

"Not important at the moment." Liza took a deep breath, preparing to say the words aloud. "I stole Gary's pickup truck. You think Huey would be interested?"

Stop sign. Brake. Heart pounding.

"Let me throw on some pants."

Blast through the intersection. "That'll take too long."

"I'm not going to Huey's without pants."

"I've got to ditch this truck before Gary catches up to me. I don't have time to collect passengers."

"You're not going to Huey's without me. A nice girl like you? He's going to assume you're a cop if I'm not there to vouch for your naiveté."

"I'm not naive."

"Maybe not if you've finally left Gary."

"I have. And better than that, I took his beloved truck. Why would Huey be worried about cops?"

"The nature of his business. Besides, things are a little touchy right now, Chiquita. I'm not saying he is, but he might be under investigation."

"Fine." Liza headed for the highway. "We'll be fast. In and out. Just like we're going to be when I stop at yours."

"What makes you think I'm not staying over someone else's?"

"Oh, sorry. Are you at someone's place?"

A wounded, "No."

"See you in twenty."

"Wait!"

"What?"

"Deep breath. Breathe with me, Liza."

"I don't have time for this."

"You get in an accident, Gary's going to find your ass."

She clenched her teeth. Forced them apart. "Fine. Deep breath. There. Bye."

"Liza Lee! This is serious."

"If I don't drop this truck at Louie's so he can make it disappear, Gary is going to kill me. That's what's serious."

"It's not Louie, it's Huey."

"Congratulations. You're in charge of introductions."

Oscar chided, "If you don't breathe deeply and center yourself, Liza, you're just asking for trouble."

"Trouble. Right."

"Liza Lee."

"Fine."

"Breathe in through your nose and hold."

Liza inhaled and held.

"Two, three, four. Exhale through your mouth."

Liza exhaled. "We done?"

"Don't you feel better?"

"Every time I look at the rearview mirror and don't see Gary on his Harley, I feel better. For about a second."

"Try not to stress, Chiquita. Once you're with me, you'll be safe."

Liza laughed. "Yeah, right. Gary's twice your size."

"From what you've said, he's not going to push me aside to get to you, afraid it will rub off."

That was true, as far as it went, but if Gary pulled a gun, and there was no reason to think he wouldn't, the bullets would go right through the both of them.

"Thanks, Oscar, for everything."

"Drive safely. Kiss, kiss."

As soon as she lost the comforting sound of her friend's voice,

Liza tensed, gripping the wheel tighter. She hadn't been joking. Gary wouldn't hesitate to kill her. He loved this truck more than anything else in the world, certainly more than her.

Maybe she should have simply snuck off once Gary finally fell asleep, but after all the blows she'd endured over the last year, she wanted to hit back.

She might not even have had the courage to leave Gary if the idea of stealing his truck hadn't crystalized.

"Fuck you, Gary."

She could do this.

She was already doing this, thick in the midst.

Drop the truck at Huey's. Take whatever cash he'd give her. Get as far away from Dallas as possible. That was the plan, simple enough that nothing could go wrong.

As Liza led Oscar into the parking lot, he grabbed her arm. "Wait."

"What?" Oscar had been fast enough leaving his apartment. Had her rushing him caused Oscar to leave something critical behind? "You'll live not having your phone."

"That's Gary's truck?"

"Yeah, that's his baby. Mine, now."

"I expected something more...normal."

Liza shrugged. "He said he got some sort of deal."

"What exactly does Gary do for work?"

"Let's go, Oscar. We can talk on the way."

"Are you sure you know how to drive that thing? Your arms reach the steering wheel, your feet the pedals?"

"I drove it here, didn't I?" She pulled him along the sidewalk.

"It's a monster."

"So's Gary, and he's probably cruising the streets looking for us."

Oscar squeaked. "You didn't tell him where I live, did you?"

"I don't remember ever telling him. But just in case I did, we better hurry."

Oscar broke free and ran.

Liza unlocked the vehicle as she followed. She climbed up into the cab and started the engine.

Oscar commented on one feature after another. "I've seen fighter jet cockpits that weren't half this complicated."

"When were you ever in a fighter jet?"

"I was asked not to tell."

Liza broke away from the curb. "So how do we get to Huey's?"

Oscar took out his phone. "See? I do too need my phone. I'll take care of the directions. You just try to keep this thing from blasting out of Earth's atmosphere."

"I only hope Huey is good at staying under the radar so that Gary doesn't beat us there."

Oscar spun to face her. "Gary knows Huey?"

"I don't think so. Maybe."

"Maybe? Maybe! What's your boyfriend do for a living?"

"A, he's not my boyfriend. B, he—he helps people. I think."

"Helps people like a social worker? Like a personal shopper? Or more like personal muscle?"

"Okay, so I don't know exactly what Gary does."

"Liza Lee. You've been living with him how long?"

"It doesn't matter. Some people don't bring their work home with them."

"For all you know, the man you stole this truck from kneecaps people for a living. It matters."

"Oscar, you've being overly dramatic. Kneecapping? Why do you always assume the worst? Just because Gary doesn't tell me what he does for work, doesn't mean it's bad. Maybe he works at an animal shelter."

"An animal shelter."

She shrugged. "Sure. Maybe he hasn't told me because he thinks it makes him look sensitive. He's afraid it will ruin his tough-guy image."

"So, he compensates for his job with this truck, and proves

he's a tough guy by beating on you."

"Or he doesn't work at a shelter. Maybe he manages a Tex-Mex restaurant. Maybe he installs gutters. Who cares?"

"Liza Lee. You don't think it's strange you don't know what your significant other does for a living?"

Oscar was a lot more fun at work where he entertained her by making fun of other people. "Gary doesn't appreciate being asked personal questions."

"You mean like, 'Hey snookums, did you kill anyone at work today?' Personal questions like that?"

"Do I give you a hard time about your relationships?"

"Sweetie, you call me in the middle of the night—"

"It wasn't quite the middle."

"You call me at a quarter to the middle the night, and what do I do? I come running."

"I picked you up."

"I ran for the phone."

"It was probably under your pillow."

"I'm here because that's what best friends do for each other."

"Thank you."

"You're welcome." Oscar shook his head. "Animal shelter my ass. Take the next right."

"I'd come running if you called, Oscar."

"I know you would, Chiquita. Assuming Gary would let you go out by yourself after dark." He exhaled. "I'm sorry if that was snarky. I'm a bit scared."

"Gary's probably still asleep."

"Even if he's not, he works in an animal shelter, right?"

Liza smiled. "He takes care of the small mammals who miss their mothers."

"Worst case scenario? He pops up behind us? He probably needs your help changing the bedding in the hamster cage. Turn here."

Liza took the right. "Are we close? I can feel Gary breathing down my neck."

"It's just a couple blocks."

Used tires. Collision repair. Mufflers. Lights off and everything closed.

"Hey, Oscar. I didn't really think about this until now, but are you sure Huey's is open?"

"While I was waiting for you to pick me up, I called, and they're expecting us."

"Good." Another first-time thought. "Once we dump Gary's truck, do you think we can borrow a car from Huey? This neighborhood is dead. We're never going to be able to get a ride."

"I'm sure he'll rent you something by the hour." Oscar pointed. "That's Huey's. Go around back."

Liza drove down the alley behind Huey's and pulled into the rear lot, aiming for the open service bay door. She heard it rattle closed behind them. Safe at last.

Jumping down to the concrete, she wondered if she should bend her knees and roll.

Liza turned to see a tall man in his sixties standing under fluorescent lights. He wore short black hair, a suit that looked out of place in an autobody shop, and cowboy boots.

Oscar called out, "Huey, thanks for agreeing to see my friend here. You look good."

"This is the truck she wants chopped?" Huey looked at Liza.

"Do you know what you have here? It is an F-450 Super Duty Limited."

What she heard was dollar signs. "So, we have a deal?"

Huey turned to Oscar as he came around the vehicle. "You did not say it was a 450 SDL."

"I didn't know."

Turned back to Liza. "A truck like this is not chopped."

She waved at the vehicle. "Look at this thing. It's giant. It's beautiful. It drives like a dream. Anybody who owns one who needs parts would pay you anything to get their own truck up and running."

"There are not enough of them on the road to make chopping

57

profitable. Instead, I would sell it."

"Great." Liza grinned at Oscar. "He can sell it."

"Come back in two days."

Her head snapped forward. "What?"

"Come back in two days."

"I need to get rid of this now." She didn't want to complicate the situation by bringing up Gary. "I need cash."

"You are not storing the truck here. In two days, I will have a buyer. Good night."

Liza took a step forward. "You don't understand. You need to take this off my hands right now."

"I will be glad to. In two days."

"What do I do until then? Drive in circles around Dallas?"

A bald black man walked out of the shadows and whistled as he surveyed the truck. "Ruby red metallic. No dings, no scratches, no dents. If you do drive this around the city, do so carefully."

He ducked and weaved his wiry frame as he examined the body from different angles. "A work of art, really. How many miles?"

"I didn't notice."

Huey raised the garage door. "Bring the truck back in two days."

Liza stood her ground. "You weren't listening to me."

Oscar touched her arm. "Liza Lee. Time to go."

"And what?"

"Come on." He helped her up into the cab before walking around to his side and climbing in. "We'll come back."

Liza looked over at Huey, who raised two fingers.

She resisted the urge to do half as much, and instead started the engine and shifted into reverse.

Liza drove aimlessly through the dark city. "There's a good chance that Gary is combing the streets for us."

"Us?"

"Me. His truck."

"Liza, did you ever tell him I knew Huey?"

"Why, are you scared? Believe me, Oscar, Gary doesn't want to hear about the guys you know. He's not going to make the connection."

Oscar turned to face her. "That's not what I'm getting at, Chiquita. If Gary doesn't think we're together tonight, we can hide at my place."

Liza paused to think it through. "He knows we're best friends."

"Yeah, but at work. We've never done anything together after hours. Why would you steal his truck and bring it to me?"

"I didn't bring it to you."

"Fine. You, me, and the truck: we're all in the same place."

"I get your point. Anyway, Gary doesn't know where you live. Even if he did suspect we're together right now, he has no way to find you."

"As long as we're in this magnificent hunk of metal, we're easy to find."

"That's why I keep expecting to see Gary in the rearview mirror."

"Excuse me for asking, Chiquita, but why did you stay with him?"

"I didn't. Or haven't you noticed we're driving around in a stolen truck?"

"But you did for a long time. I know he hit you."

Liza gripped the wheel. "I didn't think it mattered."

Oscar reached over to pat her leg. "Of course, it mattered, sweetie. You matter. Even if you don't matter to yourself, you matter to me."

"Thanks, Oscar. You, too." She paused. "I'm not pathetic, you know."

"I didn't say you were."

"I don't think I deserved to be hit. I didn't take Gary's truck hoping he would catch and punish me. I'm not dysfunctional in that way."

"No argument there."

"I want out, Oscar, and I need the money Huey is going to pay me to get out."

"I'm here to help."

"Thank you." Liza returned to her earlier thoughts. "If we did hide at your place, where would we park this beast?"

"So that Gary can't see it?"

"Preferably." She grimaced. "I still can't believe Huey won't touch the car for two days."

"He probably wants to line up a buyer first."

"He runs an autobody shop. What's one more vehicle in the lot?"

"Maybe Gary has owned this truck long enough you forget how much it stands out."

"It's not like he ever drove it all that much, just enough to keep the truck in shape. He always drove his Silverado, or his Harley when he wanted to make a statement. This is my first time behind the wheel."

"You're doing great."

"This monster might cost six figures, but the wiper controls work just like the ones in the piece-of-crap car I drove in high school."

"Maybe you should offer to become a social media influencer for the dealership."

Liza laughed for what felt the first time in days. "'Is the only thing stopping you from buying an F-450 the fear of space-age technology? Take it from me. If you can drive a piece of crap, you can drive a Super Duty Limited.'"

"Yeah, I think they might decide to go in a different direction."

Still laughing, Liza glanced at the rearview mirror. "Shit."

"What?"

"Behind us."

Oscar spun in his seat. "Gary?"

"A Harley, anyway. Matching our speed. Making a statement."

"It's probably somebody else, somebody who can't see around this prehistoric beast to pass."

"I could pull over."

"And risk knocking down buildings? Just take the next turn."

"Left? Right?"

"Correct."

The motorcycle's headlight stayed centered in the mirror.

At the next intersection, Liza turned right because there were fewer obstacles at the corner.

She watched in the rearview as the Harley continued through the intersection, the roar of its exhaust echoing in the night.

Oscar faced forward. "See? It wasn't Gary."

"Or it was, and he's going up a block before circling around in front of us."

"I like my theory better."

"Preferring an outcome is just about the best way to ensure it doesn't happen."

Oscar snorted. "If you really believed that, Chiquita, you wouldn't have stolen Gary's truck."

"Maybe I want to go out in a blaze of glory."

"Not with me, you're not. I intend to live a long and empty life."

Liza frowned. "I can let you out at the next corner."

"Seriously? I'm not letting anything happen to you, sweetie. Not on my watch. The two of us together? Gary doesn't stand a chance."

Liza tapped the brake as they approached a stop sign.

The Harley crossed in front of them.

"Damn."

"Could be a coincidence."

"He's playing with us."

"Like a cat with a mouse."

Liza shifted into park. "More like a sledgehammer with an ant."

"Just go. When your life is on the line, you're allowed to proceed without stopping."

"We're driving a stolen vehicle. No way am I begging law enforcement to stop me."

"I'd rather be pulled over by the cops than by Gary."

She shook her head. "Either way, he'd get the last laugh. Even if the cops locked us up, he'd just wait until we were released."

Oscar waved forward. "There's no point in just sitting here, making it easier for him. Go, go, go."

"Shouldn't I look both ways first?"

"Not if Gary is barreling at us from one of them."

Liza shifted and slowly accelerated through the intersection. "No way is he ramming his beloved truck. Especially on a motorcycle."

"Maybe he's ready to go out in a blaze of glory."

"I don't think he knows the meaning of the words."

"Is that good or bad?"

"Is anything?" Liza took the next left, and then the one after that, before taking the next right.

"I like to think that I'm good, which means that you're good, which means that Gary is bad."

"Gary is certainly bad." Liza snuck a glance at Oscar. "What about Huey?"

"Huey is in a category by himself. Right now, he's helping good-you get away, which makes him good."

"He put me off for two days."

"Good shaded with a smidge of bad."

Liza groaned. "We drive around like this for two days, Gary is going to catch us and do some very bad things."

"We already said Gary was bad, so that's not surprising. Even if it's disappointing."

"Huey is helping us. By keeping me waiting, Huey is helping Gary."

"But he doesn't know that he's helping Gary. Huey just doesn't want to sit on the truck for two days."

"Whether Huey knows it or not, he's putting us in the same

predicament, sitting on the truck for two days. Ignorance doesn't grant him absolution."

Liza took the next right, waiting until the last second to tap the brakes before turning.

"Do you even know where you're going?"

"I'm making it harder for Gary to follow us."

"Not the same question."

"You're getting to a bit of a smidge yourself."

"I'm in this truck, too. Our fates our entwined."

"A bond broken only by death."

"Please don't put it that way."

Liza raised a finger. "We're nestled as tightly as two armadillos sharing a shell."

"I don't think that's possible. Anyway, if Gary gets one of us, he gets us both."

"Not if we run in opposite directions."

"I'm not leaving you, Chiquita."

"You don't know that until it happens."

"I know."

Liza took the next left.

"Back to my question you didn't answer. Do you know where you're going?"

"The only idea floated was your place, although I didn't hear any solutions to the parking problem."

"There's plenty of parking in that neighborhood."

"Parking where Gary won't see his truck?"

Oscar snorted. "We could park this beast on the moon, and Gary would see it."

"He finds the truck, he finds us next."

"What about a disguise? We could disguise the truck."

Liza's nearly twisted off her head. "Seriously? As what? A moped? A fire engine? An elephant?"

"It's easy to mock."

"Sorry. I'm listening. I can't wait to hear what you're thinking."

"Still a bit mocky."

"Give me a break, Oscar. You're talking about doing the impossible."

"Okay, Liza Lee. Answer me this."

"What?"

"If Gary is going to stop at nothing to get his truck back, why hasn't he called? That's the first thing I'd do. You're gone. His truck's gone. Why doesn't he pick up the phone and call, ask you what the fuck?"

Gary crossed the intersection in front of them.

"That's why. Gary's not cruising the streets searching for us. Despite all my twists and turns, he knows exactly where we are."

"What? Then why doesn't he stop us?"

"Probably too much risk of a high-speed chase that ends in the truck getting wrecked. So instead, he simply pops up in front of us, sending the message it's pointless for me to try to run." Liza sighed. "I knew it. He's tracking our every move."

Liza continued taking random lefts and rights, making U-turns that changed their direction. Easy enough to do when she had no destination in mind, not until she confirmed that dumping her phone threw Gary off their trail.

Oscar's head snapped up. "Sorry. Must have dropped off."

"I don't dare stop until I know he can't walk up to the window and knock."

"You awake enough? I can drive if you want."

"Right now, you're just helping me. You get in an accident with Gary's truck? You're dead."

"You can get in an accident too, you know."

"But then the damage to the truck is my fault, not yours." She glanced at Oscar. "I don't want to be responsible for getting you killed."

"Neither do I. In fact, I think it would be great if neither of us gets killed."

"That's the plan." Liza directed the truck up a ramp to the

highway.

"I'm sorry Huey didn't come through for you."

"Not yet anyway. Who knows? Maybe this will be better in the long run. Maybe my cut will be bigger if he sells the truck rather than chops it for parts."

"I'm sorry if it seems weird I haven't asked about your plans, but we've got time to kill."

"Two days to kill. You can probably ask me a couple thousand questions, might even help keep us awake."

"So, what happens after Huey hands you the money?"

"I get the hell away from Gary."

"There's a lot of world to choose from."

"I haven't settled on anywhere yet. Out of Dallas, certainly. I might even leave north Texas."

"Wow. Leaving north Texas? I hope you brought your passport."

"Now who's mocking?"

Oscar shifted in his seat to face her. "It's just that if you stay in Dallas, you stay a target. North Texas...you're maybe buying yourself some time. When your life is at risk, that's not when you settle for maybe."

"I'll be fine."

"Fine until you're not. Liza Lee, you want to be thinking about Oregon, New England, Canada."

"With Canada I actually would need a passport. Besides, Gary's not a patient person. If he doesn't kill me in the next few weeks, he's going to get bored with the idea."

Oscar fluttered his hands. "Liza Lee. The fact that you're hoping Gary might not murder you because he's feeling lazy doesn't fill me with warm and fuzzy. That's not how you guarantee your safety."

Liza laughed. "Guarantee? There are no guarantees. I could be on my way out of Dallas with a bag of Huey's money when I'm hit by a train."

"So don't guarantee your safety. Stack the odds in your favor.

Mark the cards. Load the dice. Don't give Gary an even break."

"That doesn't even seem possible. Honestly, it feels like the dice are loaded against me. Even now. You think I'm free of Gary? No, he's tracking my every move."

"We haven't seen him since you tossed your phone out the window. And that was good thinking."

"He bought and paid for the phone. It only makes sense he would use it against me. That's how he thinks."

"Well, you turned the tables on him."

"I suspect Gary didn't miss a beat. If he stopped announcing himself, it was only so I'll be slapped that much harder the next time he pops up."

"I've never seen this side of you. The side that says the glass is half empty, and what it contains is poison."

"You've never seen me running for my life."

"Beats going to work."

Liza shrugged. "Work is a vacation from life. You go in, complete your shift, and leave. Nice and clean."

"Not a lot of people think that way."

"My jobs have always been an oasis, no matter how much I hated them."

"That doesn't even make sense."

"It does for me." She sighed. "As messy as the drama can sometimes get, a job description is pretty straight forward. I know what to do. I know what's expected from me."

"Well then, Chiquita, whenever you get where you're going, you should find a job as soon as you can. The money Huey gives you won't last forever."

"I just need to find someone willing to pay me under the table so I'm harder to track. At least until I get a new identity." Liza smiled. "What name do you think I should use?"

"Chiquita."

"Only you get to call me that. Next."

"Oscaretta."

Liza laughed. "Not Oscarita? Oscarina?"

"That last one's not half bad."

"Not Oscar-not-oscar?"

"Now you're just being silly."

Liza slammed the brakes, throwing the two of them forward, the truck still almost clipping the Harley that cut across the intersection in front of them. "Shit."

Oscar pushed off against the dashboard. "Liza Lee, I'm beginning to think I saw this movie, and if I remember correctly, it doesn't end well."

"I was wrong. Gary wasn't tracking me. He's tracking the truck."

"Maybe you weren't wrong. Maybe he's tracking both."

She admitted the possibility. Probability. "I can throw my phone out the window, but how do I dump the truck two days before I can dump the truck?" She slapped the steering wheel. "He knows we went to Huey's."

"Not necessarily. If he's tracking location with no way to view history, and he didn't look until we left Huey's, then we're fine."

"That's two big ifs. What if neither of them are true?"

"Then we're dead."

Liza accelerated through the intersection. "Worst-case scenario? We're dead. Less worst?"

"You mean worse?"

"I guess. But saying 'worse-case' sounds like I'm saying worse than worst-case."

"On a scale of one to ten, where ten is worst."

"Level ten, we're dead. Level nine, Gary knows about Huey's. We go there again to drop off the truck—"

Oscar raised his hands. "Don't say it."

"We're dead."

"You just said we have a twenty-percent chance of ending up dead. I'm glad I didn't suggest a scale of one to five."

"A scale of one to two."

"That would be worse."

"Worst." Lisa shook her head. "You know any other guys?"

"Round and round we go. Guys in general, or guys who chop?"

"Chop. Or resell vehicles without papers."

"Sorry, but Huey filled my personal quota for shady owners of autobody shops." Oscar paused. "I did know a guy who managed a Radio Shack."

"And, what, he switched his interests from home electronics to fencing stolen vehicles? Because that would be great."

"No, probably not. But almost as good, he lived that shit. If Gary installed a tracker somewhere on this truck, I'm betting this guy could disable it."

"How do we find him?"

Oscar glanced out his window.

"Oscar?"

"I don't know."

"You were being helpful there for a minute, Oscar, filling my heart with hope for once. What do you mean you don't know how to find him?"

He turned away from the window. "Huey I just saw last week. But this guy? It's probably been five, half-a-dozen years."

"He's not on your phone?"

"I doubt it. Even if he is in my contacts, um, I don't remember his name."

"Scroll, Oscar, scroll. Read every name and imagine saying them to his face. We've got all night."

"Sounds like a long shot."

"Gary not killing us within the next forty-eight hours is a long shot. We love long shots."

"This from Miss Glass Half Empty."

"Half empty is better than empty. Empty is better than shattered, blown apart in a hail of bullets."

Oscar covered his eyes. "I suggest we never step away from the truck. That way there's less risk of your boyfriend shooting us."

"True. Which means we're not looking for somewhere safe to park while we rest." She glanced at him. "How comfortable was your nap?"

"It didn't even count as a nap."

"You snored."

Oscar sniffed. "I don't snore. People would tell me if I snored."

"I just did."

"We can't simply drive for forty-eight hours straight, Liza. We need a real plan."

"Twenty-four hours out, and then twenty-four hours back."

"With Gary tracking us the entire time."

"We can't make decisions based on what Gary may or may not do."

"Liza Lee. In case you didn't notice, this whole thing right here revolves around Gary. There is no way in which it doesn't."

"I put him behind me."

"Maybe you're in the process of putting him behind you, Chiquita, but right now I think it's fair to say he's front-and-center. Even when he's not crossing in front of us."

"I didn't leave Gary just so he could continue to run my life."

"Once you sell the truck. Once you have the money. Once you're free to leave Gary behind for good, that's when you can consider Gary out of your life. Until then, you need to think of him as just over your shoulder."

Liza shook her head. "If I allow myself to think that way, I'll be afraid to move. You have no idea what it took for me to get this far."

"We're still in Dallas."

"You know what I mean."

"No, Chiquita, I don't know what it took you to get this far. I've never experienced that kind of relationship, and I hope I never do, because I don't know if I could escape."

"I haven't escaped yet."

"No, but you're almost there. You're almost free."

Liza Lee said, "There's something that maybe I forgot to tell you."

"Good news I hope?"

"I might be pregnant."

"Dare I ask?"

"No, I'm not naming the baby after you."

He laughed. "That wasn't my question."

"It's Gary's."

"Okay. Not definitely a disaster. Does he know?"

"I'm not sure."

"Not sure he knows you're pregnant, or not sure he knows it's his?"

"Do we have to talk about this right now? I'm trying to focus on driving."

"You're the one who brought it up, Liza Lee. Besides, you now have two things that Gary thinks belong to him. The truck. The baby. The odds of him losing interest in locating you have decreased significantly."

"Believe me. Gary doesn't want the responsibility of being a father."

"That's not the same as not wanting a child. Unfortunately. Trust me, I know."

"Once Huey takes this truck off our hands, everything will be fine."

"Even if Gary cares more about the truck than the fruit of his loins, he's not going to go away just because you sold the truck. A, he won't know you sold it. B, once he does know you sold it, then it's revenge."

"That's why I need the money to run."

"Actually, Chiquita, if you're pregnant with his kid, you might be safer than if you weren't. He's not as likely to just kill you."

"Oscar, Gary doesn't want to be a father. I told you that. My being pregnant is not going to protect me. The threat of having to raise a child might only increase the likelihood that Gary pulls the trigger."

"Let's be logical about this. A little less reactive. What's something you can hold over Gary's head?"

"Like a bargaining chip? We've got his precious truck."

"Right. If he doesn't want to risk damaging his truck, he's limited in how he can stop us. We don't have to worry about getting rammed or forced off the road." Oscar paused. "Once you sell the truck, though, what shields you then?"

"The money."

Oscar shook his head. "The money only helps you run, helps you hide. It doesn't stop Gary from hunting you down."

"Nothing is going to do that."

"More positivity, please."

"He's going to get bored."

"Less fantasy, more realistic."

"He's got to find me first."

"That's what your safety boils down to. Unfortunately, he seems to be doing well tracking you down to this point. Maybe it will change once you sell the truck and he can't track you through it. Of course, solving that problem creates new problems."

"Such as?"

"Any money you receive from selling Gary's truck just gives him more reason to catch up with you. He's going to think of it as his. The truck's gone? The money gives him just as much reason to track you down."

"The fox is running for its lunch, but the rabbit is running for its life."

"And Gary is going to be fueled by wounded male pride. I mean, Liza Lee, he has got to be pissed."

"I don't care."

"You had better care. This is your life we're talking about."

"I'm just too tired. I need to stop before I fall asleep behind the wheel. Find me a parking lot."

"Public? Private? Multi-level parking garage?"

"I don't care."

"Okay." Oscar tapped at his phone. "One cave to safely rest your head, coming up."

"We're in the middle of a car chase, Oscar."

"I prefer to think we're killing time."

"We're in the middle of a car chase, and I'm stopping to take a nap. What kind of sense does that make?"

"And so we transition from fox and rabbit to tortoise and hare."

Liza rubbed her eyes. "The hare naps and wins?"

"Close. The hare naps and loses."

"I don't care very much for that version of the story, Oscar. I vote the fox eats the tortoise, and everybody leaves the bunny alone."

"That's the version I'll read to you then."

"Thank you."

"Okay, I found you a hidey hole. Go straight through the next three intersections, and then take a right."

"Remind me again once we get closer. Good job finding us somewhere to take a break."

Oscar blew her a kiss. "You're welcome."

Liza jerked awake.

Where were they?

The parking lot Oscar found.

Oscar, snoring softly in the seat next to her.

Liza shifted. Stretched. Sighted a flip phone centered on the hood of the trunk.

She leaned forward to examine it more closely.

Yes, a flip phone.

Liza glanced out each window, craning her neck to search for any sign of Gary or his Harley. Or any other possible threat. But who else would leave her a phone?

Liza shook Oscar awake.

"Wha?"

"There's a phone on the hood."

Oscar rubbed his eyes. "There's what?"

"I'm going to go out and get it. If anything strange happens, blast the horn."

Blinking, he studied the steering wheel in the half-light. "How do I do that?"

"You'll figure it out." Liza unlocked her door and opened it just wide enough to drop down to the lot. She glanced around before darting to the front of the truck.

She couldn't reach the phone.

Liza dashed back and climbed into the cab. "Hold on."

"Why?"

She started the engine, pressed the accelerator, and then stomped on the brake.

The phone slid across the hood and went over the edge. "I'll be back."

"I'll keep looking for the horn."

Liza retrieved the phone and climbed back into the cab, locking her door behind her. She flipped back the cover of the phone, the screen bright. "I don't think it's broken."

"That's good in a phone."

There was one contact entered.

Liza glanced at Oscar. "Gary's number is in here. Should I call him, or wait for him to call me?"

"Call him and get it over with."

She started the truck again. "I want to move first."

"What's the point? He'll know wherever we are as soon as we're there."

"Still." Liza pulled out of the lot. "Get me on the highway. Please."

"Any highway in particular?"

"Thirty-five."

"North or south?"

"Towards Oklahoma. Gary's not going to expect that."

"He's tracking us. He's tracking the truck. He's probably tracking the phone."

"Yes, but he might have already started south in order to be ahead of us. Going north gives us a slight advantage."

"Any advantage is good. North it is."

Liza drove in silence, turning the wheel to follow Oscar's instructions, accelerating whenever the road in front of them was straight.

"It could be worse, you know."

Lisa snorted. "How?"

"The phone could have three numbers programmed in. Gary's, mine, and Huey's."

"Okay, so that would be worse." She turned to face Oscar. "Don't credit Gary with being all-knowing, all-powerful. He's just your average prick. We can beat him."

"I'm trying to stay positive, Chiquita. Gary is just a man. If he beats me to within an inch of my life, will his knuckles not bleed?"

"I'm not sure if that's being positive."

"If he slits my throat, will he not have to wipe the blade?"

Liza shook her head. "I think I'll just focus on driving."

"If he shoots me to death, will he not need to reload?"

"You can stop now."

Oscar lowered his phone. "How much longer do you plan to drive before you call him?"

"This is me, delaying the inevitable."

"Why? Maybe he's offering another way out."

"That's not his style."

"When we were stopped, he could have disabled the truck without damaging it. He could have let the air out of the tires. He could have blocked us in. Instead, he left you the phone. He wants to talk."

"Don't take his side, Oscar."

"Don't? I'm not. I'm trying to keep us alive, and if Gary might be willing to compromise on how dead he wants us, I'm willing to listen."

"Then you call him."

"He doesn't want to talk to me."

"True. But I don't want to talk to him."

Oscar leaned towards her. "You're strong enough to listen to Gary on the phone, hear him out. Nothing he can say will hurt you. Nothing he can say will make you go back."

"I don't want to listen to his bullshit."

"The fact that you know it's bullshit gives you an edge, Liza Lee. Gary might think he's playing you, but you're actually playing him."

"I just want to be done with it. Done with it all."

"You will, Chiquita. You will. We just need to stay alive long enough to sell this monster so that you can get the money and take off. Will talking to Gary on the phone help? We don't know."

"I know I don't want to talk to him."

"But if it helps you in the long run?"

"Okay, you win."

"Chiquita, I'm on your side."

"Find us a place to pull over."

"It's you and me against Gary. The only win that counts is when you get safely away."

"I'm not even sure how that looks anymore."

"It looks like you going to work, happy to be there, going back to wherever you're living, happy to be there, content to be on your own."

"Seems like a dream. Which makes sense because I feel like I'm still half asleep."

"Take the next left. Someday soon, the time you spent with Gary will seem the dream, a little harder to remember every day."

"Not if he catches up with us first."

"He won't. And if it looks like he might, we'll figure a way through."

Liza took the left. "Where is Oscar in this fantasy of yours?"

"It sounds strange, but this is the most time we've spent to-gether outside work."

"Seriously?"

"I shit you not."

Liza laughed. "I've always gotten a kick out of that phrase."

"We were co-workers long before we were friends."

"But now we're friends."

"No doubt." Said not as strongly as Liza expected.

"I mean it, Oscar. You're probably my best friend. Who's your best friend?"

"I wouldn't even know how to answer that. Look at us. We have a work friendship. We're fighting the same fight working for the same people. We have the same enemies."

"We laugh at the same things. The same people."

"Peter."

The two burst into laughter, a laughter magnified by exhaustion and fear.

Liza managed to stop laughing first. "I hear what you're saying about work friends, Oscar, but I think we're more than that. There's no one else I wanted to tell I left Gary. Once I settle in somewhere, there's no one else I want to show off the place to."

"It's not that I don't want you to make new friends."

"Assuming you know to bring a house-warming gift."

"After you sell this truck, you're going to be the one with all the money."

"So make me something. Steal me something from work."

"But that would be wrong."

"Like what we're doing here is right."

"That's different. Gary hits you. Stealing his truck, we're letting him off easy."

"He catches us, he's going to think a beating is letting us off easy. You might believe I should have done more to stand up for myself, but you have no idea what it's like living with him."

"I'm not criticizing you."

"It sure sounded that way to me."

"I'm not." Oscar took a deep breath. "I guess I'm trying to justify what we're doing."

"You're having second thoughts? I thought you were my friend."

"I am. That's why I'm helping you. But being your friend doesn't mean ignoring my conscience."

"I didn't realize I was creating an existential crisis."

"That's not what I meant, either." Oscar shook his head. "Forget I said anything."

"No, Oscar, I want to know exactly what coming along on this adventure is costing you. What it's costing me."

"Nothing. That's not how it works, Liza Lee. Friends don't keep ledgers."

"I don't know. You say that, but it sounds like you do."

"Where's this coming from? Are you spoiling for a fight?"

"You brought it up."

"What, my conscience?"

"Either you're in this all the way, or you're not."

"Do you see me sitting right beside you? That should put any of your doubts to rest."

"That's just it. Until a few minutes ago, I thought we were on the same page."

"We are."

"Except that stealing Gary's truck gets me out of a horrible situation and ruins the rest of your life."

"I don't suppose it would be helpful to say you're overreacting."

"Maybe I am. Maybe I'm just tired. I know I'm tired. I'm exhausted and irritable."

"Understandable." He patted her leg. "The good news is, we're almost done with this."

"How can you even say that? Huey won't take the car for two days. We're not even through the first night."

"Not yet we aren't, but we will be. You'll see. This will be over before you know. Turn left up here."

"You're not going to let me give up, are you?"

"That's not what friends do."

"You're always there for me, Oscar." Liza took the left into a parking lot. "I never forget that, and I never will."

"That goes double for me."

She pulled into the first empty spot, shifted into park, and raised the phone. "Here goes nothing."

"We can hope."

Gary answered on the first ring. "Having fun?"

His voice sent a chill through her body. "Not particularly."

"They call it a joy ride, babe. You're supposed to have fun."

"This is goodbye, Gary."

Gary snorted. "You don't want to make any statements you can't walk back, babe. That's a dangerous approach."

"I don't need to walk it back because it's true."

"What does that even mean? You need to come home."

"I'm done. I'm done with you. I'm done with us."

"Here's what's true. You need to return that truck. Now."

"Consider it restitution."

Gary laughed. "No, babe, that's not how this works. Here's how this works. You bring back the truck."

"And then what?"

"If you want to leave, leave."

Liza shook her head. "I don't believe that for a second."

"You don't want to be here, I'll find somebody who does. I just need that truck."

"So do I."

"You don't understand." Gary drew a ragged breath. "I need that truck."

"This truck is my ticket out of town."

"You're not listening to me, babe."

"I'm listening."

"Then you're not hearing me. *Hablo ingles?* Bring. Me. The. Truck."

Liza grimaced. "How many times did you hit me I didn't call the cops? I never called the cops. You owe me."

"You're taking the truck as payment?" Gary snorted. "Guess what, babe? It's not even mine."

Pieces fell into place even as her plan shattered. "What do

mean it's not yours?"

"They're releasing Slick tomorrow."

Liza's blood went cold. "So?"

"Guess what's the first thing he's going to do after carving the guy who snitched."

"I don't know."

Gary nearly whispered, "He's going to collect the truck I've been holding for him."

"You're lying."

"You wish. Five minutes after Slick learns you stole his truck, he's going to kill me, you, and your little friend there. But you. Slick is going to take his time with you. Slick discovers you stole his truck, he's going to skin you alive and make pork rinds."

Liza closed her eyes. If Gary was telling the truth about the truck, being skinned alive was probably the best-case scenario.

They said Slick smiled when he was sentenced, and the judge who slapped him with the two-year maximum for a state felony was killed in a hit-and-run three days later.

Coincidence? Nobody thought so, but nothing could be proved. Nobody was even ever questioned.

Liza shivered. If this truck was Slick's, and that possibility made a certain amount of sense, it was also her death warrant.

Fuck it. She needed this truck if she was going to break free. She'd earned it.

Liza closed the phone's lid, ending the call.

Liza summarized the call with Gary as, "We need to keep moving, Oscar."

"I need more than that, Chiquita. All I could hear was your side of the conversation, and I don't feel completely caught up."

"Gary wants the truck back."

"That shouldn't come as a surprise. What else did he say?"

Liza took a deep breath. "So, you know how I said I was taking Gary's truck as payment?"

"I don't remember you using those exact words. I thought getting money from Huey was the objective."

"It is." Liza lowered her window and sent the phone sailing. "But taking Gary's truck is also a way of getting back at him. It's like the perfect revenge."

"Two for one. Good going!"

"Not so fast with the congratulations there, partner. Gary just told me the truck isn't his."

"You stole a stolen vehicle? At least he can't report it, add the cops to our woes."

"Don't get excited, Oscar. According to Gary, he was holding the truck for someone else. That's why he babied it. The guy who owns the truck, he's being released tomorrow."

"Released from the hospital?"

Liza laughed. "Yeah. He's such a sweet person, it was messing with his blood sugar levels. I wish. No, the guy who owns the truck isn't going to hand us lollipops for filling the tank."

"I never liked lollipops, to be honest."

"Gary talks a lot of shit. He's always going to do this to that person, do that to the other guy first. You know."

"Yeah, I'm the same way. Totally. So, who owns the truck?"

"The one exception to Gary's macho persona is Slick."

Oscar paused. "You're probably talking about another Slick."

"I'm afraid not."

"I bet the Slick who owns this truck is the nicest guy you'll ever meet. In fact, I'm sure of it. Liza, my skin is drier than I would like, but I would prefer to keep it on my body. How many people live in the greater Dallas metropolitan area? There must be dozens of people called Slick. Hundreds."

"So, yeah, now Gary is the least of our concerns."

"What's worse than worst-case scenario? This is. That's what's worse. Worst. Whatever."

"Gary's not going to tell Slick we took his truck."

"What's his option? Find a replacement? You heard Huey. There are none to be had."

"But if Gary's one job was to protect Slick's truck, and Gary blew that? Your boyfriend can't risk telling the truth."

"He's not my boyfriend, and never was. But you're right, he can't tell the truth. He has to get this truck back. Whatever it takes."

Oscar raised a hand. "You said Slick was being released. When?"

"What's it matter? Slick doesn't even know we have his truck."

"Liza Lee, when is Slick being released?"

"Tomorrow."

"Tomorrow, or, because it's after midnight, today?"

"And you give me a hard time for being glass-half-empty."

"So today. When exactly? First thing in the morning, or late in the afternoon?"

"What do I look like, a prison warden? Slick is released when they release him. First, he's going to talk to Gary, and Gary is going to spin some bullshit story because he doesn't want to die, either."

"Maybe if I beg Huey to speed things up."

"That would be great."

"Then again Huey might not want to touch this deal if he knows the truck actually belongs to Slick because Huey appreciates having skin as much as anyone else."

"So don't tell him."

"We want me to just not mention that he's negotiating the sale of Slick's truck."

"Exactly. Huey doesn't need to know that."

"I'm sure he's going to think differently."

"Huey is just the middleman, connecting two parties for a commission. We don't even have to make the exchange at his shop. We can meet the buyer elsewhere."

"Huey is going to want to know. The buyer is going to want to know. You take this truck to a car wash, they're going to want to know they're going to die if they leave water spots."

"Once it's chopped, nobody is going to care. It'll be too late.

The parts will be spread all over."

"But Huey isn't chopping it, Chiquita. He's negotiating a sale."

She licked her lips. "That's right. I forgot my original plan fell through. But that doesn't mean we can't pretend it's still on."

"What do you mean?"

"Huey knows he's selling it, and so we don't mention Slick, risk sabotaging the deal. We then tell Gary it was chopped, and he reports the same to Slick. There's no reason to track us down. The truck's gone."

"That sounds very glass half full of you, but do you really expect Gary to just let bygones be bygones? Slick certainly won't."

"I'm not returning the truck to Gary. End of story. This is my Alamo."

"You couldn't pick a metaphor where everybody lived? Fine. At least we know where we stand. Even if it's our last stand."

"Once we get rid of the truck, Slick is Gary's problem, not mine. We're free of them both, Oscar."

"Your cup is not only half full, it sounds as though it's over-flowing without spilling a drop. I know you're exhausted, but don't you think it's just possible that Gary will rat you out to save himself?"

"There's no way Gary can spin this without looking bad."

"Better to look bad than be skinned alive, Liza Lee."

"From everything I've heard about Slick, he's not going come out of prison saying he found Jesus. Not unless there was some guy named Jesus serving five years who once tried to cross Slick, and who somehow managed to flush himself down a prison toilet."

"Um. I think you're making my point."

"Am I? All I know is I want to get rid of this truck as soon as possible. Gary's out there. Slick's going to be out there soon. The longer we're driving around, the emptier that glass becomes."

"Maybe we should just dump it somewhere."

"You're joking."

"I don't think either of us wants to die out here."

"Maybe you should call Huey and tell him he's got three hours to line up a buyer or we're going somewhere else."

"That's not—"

"If he tells you any whiff of desperation will drive down the price, tell him I don't care. Tell him to double his cut."

"This isn't a good idea. You don't rush people like Huey."

"I'm making this a seller's market. Tell him if he can't make the deadline, we'll go somewhere else."

"There is nowhere else."

"Huey doesn't need to know the details. Just act as though we have options."

"Liza Lee, Huey knows his line of work. Anybody else doing what Huey does, he knows who they are. You start floating the idea you've got another deal lined up, he's going to make calls."

"If he has time to make calls, he's got time to find me a buyer. If not, we'll just find someone ourselves."

Oscar covered his eyes. "Great. So now the plan is we drive around until we see the sign: 'We Sell Used Trucks. Certified stolen.' That's not a plan, Liza Lee, not with Gary breathing down our neck."

"How is that not a plan?"

Oscar removed his hands. "Hoping for a miracle? Hoping for a miracle is not a plan."

"Fine. Convince Huey to take this truck off my hands. There's your plan. There's your task."

"I have to tell Huey to produce a buyer out of thin air in less than three hours, and if we can't, we're going to die."

"Pretty much."

"Chiquita. I should never have picked up the phone."

"You had to. We're best friends."

"Best friends don't get each other killed."

"That's why you have to call Huey."

"So now it's my fault if Slick skins us alive."

"That's not what I said. But if it helps motivate you, yes."

Oscar shook his head. "When you called me earlier, all you wanted from me was Huey's name. You've now escalated the situation to where what I do determines whether we live or die."

"No pressure."

"None at all." Oscar cleared his throat. "Any tips before I call him?"

"Don't forget to say please."

Oscar scrolled, and then stopped. "Wait a second."

"We don't have time to wait."

"About your pregnancy." Oscar tapped the phone against his upper lip.

"What?"

"There's got to be a way it helps our situation."

"I don't see how."

"I don't either, yet. But we have to be able to turn it to our advantage."

"Just make the call, Oscar. If we can convince Huey to take the truck from us now, we don't have to say I'm pregnant."

"I'm not suggesting we promise anybody the child."

"Make the call, Oscar."

"Fine." He resumed scrolling, and then tapped.

A few seconds later, he said, "Hey, Huey. It's Oscar. I hope I didn't wake you."

A murmur from the phone.

"Right, well, we were wondering if you'd found a buyer yet."

The murmur.

"I know. It's just my friend is really motivated to sell. Time is of the essence, and all that. She knows it's a lot to ask."

Murmur.

"Yes, she knows it's going to cost."

Oscar nodded as Huey continued to murmur.

Liza took a hand from the wheel to slap his leg, whispering, "Three hours. Don't forget the deadline."

Oscar brushed her hand away, continuing to nod, continuing to listen to Huey, who obviously continued to talk.

Finally, Oscar said, "Yes. Thank you." Disconnected as he took a deep breath.

"Well?"

"Huh?" Oscar lowered the phone.

"Huey. What did he say?"

"He'll try."

"Oscar, Huey said more than 'He'll try,' unless he repeated it eighty-seven hundred times."

"The good news is that Huey doesn't skin people. The bad news is he isn't happy."

"You didn't even tell him about the three-hour deadline."

"Yeah. I got a very strong impression that your ask would not be well received."

"It's more than an ask, Oscar. We need to unload this vehicle."

"As Huey would say—as Huey did say—that's not his problem. Even suggesting we need to move up the timetable makes him nervous, and people like Huey don't like to be made nervous."

"So, what, he's bailing on us?"

Oscar shook his head. "Huey is talking to a potential buyer."

"Great. Then he can take the truck off our hands and front me the money."

"That's not how this works, Chiquita."

"Oscar, don't keep telling me how this works. I know how it works. I hand the keys to Huey. Huey hands the money to me. I'm gone. I don't want to die any more than you do."

"Which is zero."

"Right. How we don't die is we unload this truck."

"I'm not sure that's any guarantee of our safety, wounded egos and all, but let's be half full and assume you're right, Liza Lee. We still can't unload the vehicle until Huey lines up a buyer."

"I didn't even want to sell it. Remember? I wanted a simple exchange. I give Huey a truck to chop. He hands me a bag of money."

"Yeah, well, the truck you stole was too valuable for that to happen."

"So now it's my fault."

"No, it's Gary's or Slick's. Slick for buying it. Slick for trusting it with Gary. Gary for letting you waltz off with the vehicle in the middle of the night."

"Gary didn't let me 'waltz' off. I put a lot of thought into how I was going to do this. I took a big chance."

"I didn't mean to belittle The Great Dallas Truck Robbery. I'm just saying it's not your fault. Which was your point. I was agreeing with you."

"Oscar, I just—If Huey can't take this truck off our hands this morning, he's forcing us to go elsewhere. I don't know anybody else who owns a chop shop. You say you don't know anybody else. Where does that leave us?"

"I don't know."

"We could try a pawnbroker. Maybe that person knows somebody who knows somebody, but we're going to get ripped off."

"As opposed to Huey, who has a reputation for honesty."

"He's letting me down, but yes, you said I could trust him." Liza shook her head. "I don't know if I can wait for him to come through."

"Maybe you can't afford not to."

She groaned. "Gary's out there, and he knows exactly where we are. Come the dawn, Slick's going to be out there."

"Even if they release first thing in the morning, there's paper-work and tearful goodbyes. Slick's a problem...noon at the earliest."

"Thanks, Oscar, for that reassurance." She paused. "Who was that other guy?"

"What other guy?"

"At Huey's shop. The black guy who fell in love with the truck."

"I don't know."

"You think maybe he'd be interested in a side deal?"

"You mean ask him to go behind Huey's back?"

"Huey's not moving fast enough."

"I don't think you want to go there, Liza Lee."

"Maybe this other guy knows people Huey doesn't. Maybe he knows a guy who knows a guy who moves trucks overseas, cash on the hood."

"You can't even reach the hood. You had to wrench out my spine getting that phone off the hood."

"So, skip the hood. He hands me the money, hands me the gym bag. My point is: the guy who works at Huey's could be our ticket forward."

"And, what? You want me to call Huey and ask him to put the other guy on? Ask the other guy to step outside so Huey can't overhear?"

"That could work."

Oscar huffed. "I'm glad to see you've managed to keep your sense of humor through all this."

"Cry and you cry alone."

"Not if I'm with you."

"Thanks, Oscar." She blew him a kiss. "But seriously, we need to find a way through this. What was the name of the guy who worked at Radio Shack?"

"I told you, I don't remember."

Liza shrugged. "I hoped if I surprised you with the question, the name would come back."

"Sorry, but it didn't."

"Okay, you know lots of people. Who else might be able to help us?"

"In what way?"

"In any way at this point. Someone who chops. Someone who sells cars. Someone who can get us a gun. Someone with good snacks because I am starving."

"A gun? I don't think we want to go there, Liza Lee. This thing escalates into a shootout, I'll tell you right now who ends up dead."

"Fine. Forget defending ourselves."

"We're defending ourselves with your wit and determination."

"I'd rather have a bundle of money."

"Huey is going to come through. You just have to be patient."

Liza shook her head. "We need to think outside the box. Outside the country. We need to find someone who moves cars into Mexico, or Canada, or the Middle East even. This truck we're sitting on is a prime piece of Grade A, all-American engineering. Who wouldn't want one?"

"Anybody who sees the price tag."

"Rich people are everywhere, Oscar, and they all love their vehicles. At least this beast is about more than appearances. Hell, after driving it tonight, I'd make an offer if I had the money."

He sniffed. "If you had the money, you wouldn't have had to steal it."

Liza grinned. "I might have stolen it anyway, just to see the look on Gary's face."

"Which you didn't see."

"In my mind. I saw the look on his face in my mind. I just know he lost his shit. That alone makes this worthwhile."

"Wait a second."

"What?"

"There was a woman, always wore her hair in a pony. Had a blue streak down the middle. I could never figure out how she always got it exactly down the middle. The pony's on the back of her head!"

"What about her?"

"She ran a string of waypoints for one of the cartels. She always drove a big truck."

"That's good. Even if she's not in the market, she might know someone who is. What's her name?"

"Give me time, Chiquita. I can't work miracles."

"Time is not something we have to spare."

"What about you, Liza Lee? You haven't spent the last twenty years locked in a tower. Who do you know?"

"I know you. Isn't that enough?"

"I should be enough for anybody."

"More than enough."

"Thank you."

"But to answer your question, Gary keeps me on a tight leash. Probably the only reason he lets me work is because it's legal money."

"And you get to spend time with me."

"Not really one of Gary's priorities. So this woman. Do you remember her name any better than Mr. Radio Shack's?"

"No."

"Oscar, you're being less than helpful."

"Don't be so quick to judge, Chiquita. I do remember how she organized her waypoints."

"I'm listening."

"She manages several tow companies that also provide highway repairs for big rigs." Oscar crossed his arms with an element of smug. "The nearest shop is in Waxahachie."

"Get me some directions."

Oscar whipped out his phone. "I'll take that as a 'thank you.'"

"Take it any way you want. Just get us there."

"A 'please' wouldn't be rejected out of hand."

"Neither would a lead that actually panned out."

Shaking his head, Oscar muttered, "Some people are just ungrateful."

"Some people don't want to die."

Oscar crowed. "Found the shop, and we are locked in on target."

"Tell me when to turn."

"Navigator to pilot, roger that."

Liza laughed. "I'm going to miss you, Oscar."

"You don't have to disappear off the face of the earth, you know. You just have to be somewhere Gary wouldn't look."

"Until he stops looking, and then I'll be free."

"How exactly are you going to know when that happens? It's

not like he's going to text you that he gives up. And Slick, don't forget about Slick."

"I can't."

"Slick might have better concentration than your boyfriend."

"Most people do."

"If Slick's the type to not quit until he gets satisfaction, he's not likely to simply let this go."

"He skins people." Liza snorted. "I think that's about all you need to know to understand where Slick stands on the forgiveness scale."

"Here's an idea. Give Slick his truck back. You already made clear to Gary how you feel. It sounds as though he's okay with you leaving, and if anything, he's going to owe you for returning Slick's truck."

"I want the money. It's that simple."

"I assume you also want your skin."

"Let me ask you a question, Oscar."

"Go ahead."

"Why are you still here? You made the introduction to Huey. That's all I asked from you."

"Because I'm your friend. I want to make sure you come out on the other side of this in one piece."

"Is that all?"

"What do you mean?"

"I don't know. You tell me."

"Take the next exit. Loop over and get back on the highway headed south." Oscar lowered the phone. "I don't understand what you're getting at."

"I guess: what's in it for you?"

"Um. We're friends?"

"We're work friends. While I'm not dismissing that, or minimizing how much your friendship means to me, being in this truck could get you killed. Horribly."

"I try not to think about that."

"Maybe you should."

"I don't understand where you're going with this. Are you trying to get rid of me? Do you want me gone? Maybe you want to drop me off at the next all-night convenience store?"

"No, that's not what I'm saying. I just want to know what's in it for you."

"You never heard of friendship?"

"Sure, but there's got to me more."

"Why?"

"Because your life is on the line. If Gary doesn't kill you, Slick will."

"I don't see you calling it quits."

"That's because my eye is on the prize. Is it the money? Do you expect to get a piece of the money?"

"No."

"Because if that's what you're thinking, you need to stop right now. I need that money to get the hell out of here, to start again fresh."

"I got that, Chiquita."

"I wish I could believe you."

Oscar's head snapped back. "So now I'm a liar?"

"Your words, not mine."

"Your implication. I certainly did not see this coming. Next, you're going to accuse me of asking Huey to drag this out."

"The thought did cross my mind."

"Seriously?"

"I only have your word on what you told him on the phone."

"We should just agree to drop this."

"Fine."

"We're tired. We're being hunted. Something we thought was going to be easily proved to be more complicated. Anyway, I'm not expecting to receive a cut."

Liza took a deep breath. "You've probably earned one, a finder's fee. You're the one who brought me to Huey."

"You need the money more than I do. I'm not the one with a Gary."

Liza swore.

"What?"

"Speaking of needing money, we're almost out of gas. At least it will give me an excuse to get out of truck and walk around some. As comfortable as this seat is, I wouldn't mind a good stretch."

"I'll search for a station that's open."

"I guess it only makes sense we're burning gas, all this driving around, but now I'm spending money on the truck instead of making money."

"You just have to hold it together for another few hours and then you can run across an open field waving fistfuls of cash."

"Assuming Huey comes through."

"Selling this truck helps him, too. Don't forget that. He'd be a fool to settle for a low-ball first offer."

"The longer this takes, the more this costs me. The more it takes out of me."

"You're just tired."

"That's what I'm saying. I can imagine being so done with this that I decide to forget the whole thing, drive back home, and crawl into Gary's bed. Not that I'm going to do it. I can just see it play out that way in my mind."

"Maybe when we stop for gas, you should get something to eat. Maybe we should walk around the station a few times. A body in motion tends to lift your emotion."

"I thought a body in motion was harder to stop."

"I'm sure it's a lot of things. Stay in this lane. You're going to turn right in a few minutes."

"What are we doing, Oscar?"

"Getting off the highway to get gas."

"No, I mean big picture."

"Getting you out of Dallas."

"You can take the girl out of Dallas, but does she ever really escape?" Liza snorted. "I'm glad you didn't say we were wasting time until time won."

"Maybe you should buy some chocolate. Yes, you could definitely use some chocolate."

"Let's be honest, Oscar. What does it even mean to be free? What if I just end up with another Gary?"

"You won't. You know better now." Oscar pointed. "This is our right up ahead. The thing about another Gary is, you'll recognize the warning signs. You'll know to run in the opposite direction."

"But what if I'm attracted to men like Gary?"

"That was the old you. This is the new you, the wiser you."

"Maybe. Mistakes have a habit of repeating. Mistakes are a habit."

"You simply replace the bad habit with a newer one. Like spending the money you're going to make by selling this truck on exercise equipment or a juicer."

She took the exit and slowed as they approached a crossroad. "Which way do we turn?"

"You don't see it?" Oscar pointed at a gas station, outlined by Christmas lights.

"I'm tired. Leave me alone."

"You're going to create a habit of taking better care of yourself. Of celebrating yourself."

Liza sighed. "Do you really think that's possible?"

"It has to be, or what's the point?"

"Of getting away from Gary?"

"Of anything."

Liza pulled next to the pumps, parked, and went inside for snacks. Standing at the register, she glanced through the window to see Oscar's face shining in the light from his phone.

"That be all?"

"Yes, thank you." The store was unnaturally bright.

The clerk said she could insert her card while placing the random items she'd grabbed in a plastic bag.

Liza walked back to the truck at an angle, causing Oscar to jump when she knocked on his window.

He opened the door, and she handed him the bag.

She inserted her charge card into the pump and selected the lowest grade of gas.

Then she pumped. And pumped. And pumped.

She almost looked under the truck to see if the gas was collecting below.

The dials finally stopped spinning after she'd pumped forty-six gallons.

Liza swore before she replaced the nozzle.

Then she walked around the truck, opened the door, and climbed in. "I don't know how big the gas tank on this beast is, but I think it's larger than my last car."

Oscar swiveled to read the pump. "Wow."

She started the truck. "Next time, you're paying."

"If things go according to plan, there won't be a next time."

"Let's hope not."

Oscar raised a finger. "Hope not, or hope so?"

"Worse than worst."

"Half-filled is half empty."

Liza pulled out of the gas station. "I should have settled for half-filled, but I couldn't stop pumping."

"Better than having to stop again later."

"Watching the dials spin was like watching a train wreck in slow motion."

"I'm sure you don't want to hear this, but I had a lot of time to kill while you were pumping gas."

"Hit me."

"I searched for used pickup trucks."

"And?"

"There are no other trucks like this being sold for hundreds of miles. In fact, I couldn't find one being sold anywhere in the country."

"And?"

"When there are only two dots to connect, anybody can draw the line and see the picture. We've got two dots. This truck for sale. Slick owning this exact make, model, and year."

"By the time he hears anything, we'll be long gone."

"Also, I called in sick tomorrow. I was scheduled."

"I can understand you not wanting to go in after being up all night."

"Especially if Gary kills me. Or Slick does worse."

"Worst would be having to work anyway." She threw him a grin. "Of course, you could always come with me."

"You don't even know where that is."

"So, help me find it."

"I'll miss you, Liza, but I have a life here, shitty as it is. I've got family. I've got friends. Those friends are not as important to me as you are, but they don't need to know that."

"Oscar has family?"

"Why wouldn't I?"

"I don't know. I just always saw you as self-contained. I always imagined that one day you simply appeared out of the hills."

"I'm betting even Liza has a family."

"Not so you'd notice." She glanced at his phone. "Don't you have any directions for me?"

"Go with God, my child."

Lisa laughed. "I've got the Devil in the rearview, so why not?"

"I noticed how you change the subject when I brought up your family. If you don't want to talk about them, that's fine."

"Good."

"I won't ask any questions."

"Glad to hear it."

"I won't even pester you for details."

"If you're wondering whether anybody will grieve me, the answer is no."

Oscar waved. "Hello."

"You know what I meant."

"I'll be your family, Chiquita. Look what we're doing right now. Stealing a truck as a family activity."

Liza grunted. "Sure beats repainting the living room."

"Is that what you did with your family?"

"Only if blood counts."

"Well then." Oscar shifted in his seat. "What did I do with those snacks you bought?"

"You're asking me?"

Oscar rooted around on the floor. "Got it." Sat up and examined the contents. "You couldn't make up your mind."

"I wasn't sure how much longer we were going to be driving around."

"Hopefully not long enough to eat all this." He turned to face her. "What do you want?"

"Something chocolate."

He peeled open a candy bar and handed it to her. "I'm going to have spice drops."

"I bought spice drops?"

"Bought them. Stole them." Oscar shrugged. "They're in the bag."

"Huh." Liza bit off a piece of chocolate.

"This is our exit coming up."

"Entrance. It's the entrance to the highway."

"It's our exit off this road."

"Half empty."

"Half full."

"The line that divides them." Liza veered onto the ramp.

"Ooh, lemony."

Liza shook her head. "I can't believe I actually bought spice drops."

"You're a better person than you thought."

"Nobody is a better person than they think they are. They're worse. Always."

"I think maybe someone could use a spice drop."

"Not on your life." Reaching the highway, Liza floored the accelerator and whipped into the passing lane. "Only one thing is going to improve my attitude, and I'm sure you know what it is."

Oscar sighed. "Being handed a stack of money for this truck."

"That's all I ask."

"I assume you'd rather not get killed by Gary."

"The money will keep that from happening."

"Maybe."

"Fine. I'll keep that from happening, but to succeed, I need the money."

"Fair enough."

She stole a glance at him. "Why do I get the sense you think I'm making a mistake?"

"I don't. I'm glad you left Gary."

"But."

"There's no 'but.' I'm honestly glad."

"But you think it was a mistake to steal this truck."

"I don't know if it was the wisest move to steal a truck that meant so much to him, and that's before we learned it belongs to Slick. Plus, a truck this valuable? If you'd stolen an F-150, Huey would have handed you the money when we arrived."

"Gary doesn't own an F-150."

"Gary doesn't own an F-450 Super Duty Limited, either. This is Slick's truck."

"I didn't know that. Hindsight is twenty-twenty."

"Fifty-fifty."

"So, what we have is a glass half filled, a stolen truck that's too valuable to steal."

"Who would have thought?"

"Huey might still come through. This person you're taking me to now might come through. We have options."

"That's what we hope, anyway."

"Oscar." She paused. "Am I making a mistake trusting you?"

"What? How can you even ask that?"

"You're the one who knows Huey. You're the one who knows this woman Huey put me off, and maybe this woman will as well."

"You asked for my help because I'm more social than you are. You can't turn around and then blame me for it."

"Just because I trust you enough to ask for your help, doesn't mean I can trust you. Maybe you know Gary. Maybe he made you a deal. Maybe you're just driving me around in circles until he gets tired of playing cat-and-mouse, until he decides where he'd going to dump my body."

"Liza Lee. Do you want to hurt my feelings? Is that what this is about? Push me away before you head off into the sunrise?"

"I just had to ask."

"Well, I don't need to answer. I am here for you. I am sitting right next you to you in this cab while out there Gary is hunting us, and Slick will be before long."

"We don't know that about Slick."

"You know that Gary isn't going to protect you while his skin is being flayed. You can assume that Slick isn't going to ignore what he learned, putting all that torture to waste. If Gary doesn't find us first, Slick is going to find us worst."

Liza's knuckles went white on the steering wheel. "Huey is coming through for us. Huey or this woman. We're going to be long gone by the time Slick figures out anything."

"That's another thing that sort of bothers me, Chiquita. You say 'we' are going to be safe, even though it's only you taking off with the money. People saw me with you at Huey's. Gary might even have seen me when he cut across in front of us."

"He was facing forward."

"You think. And even if Gary didn't see me himself, there was I standing next to you at Huey's."

"Are you saying Huey is going to talk?"

"If Slick starts asking questions? Huey might not be intimidated, but that doesn't mean they won't come to an agreement. You'd have to be crazy not to tell Slick anything he wanted to hear."

"So, what are you suggesting, that you're a threat to me?"

"What? No. I'm saying I'm the one in danger."

"If Slick goes after you, you can put him on me. After all, you'd have to be crazy not to tell Slick anything he wanted to hear."

"I don't even know your plans."

"But you keep asking about them as if you want to amass some bargaining chips."

"I ask because I'm your friend. I care about you. I want to know you're going to be safe."

"I need to be sure."

"Trust me, Chiquita, you can be sure."

"And what if I'm wrong? That's what I keep asking myself." She glanced at him. "I'd feel better if you were coming along with me."

"I told you. My life's here."

"Not if you're dead."

"That was my original point. You're fleeing the area. I'm the one staying behind. I'm the one at risk."

"Only if Huey talks. Or this woman we're going to see."

Oscar snapped his fingers. "Rosie. That's her name."

"Okay, Rosie. We don't know whether Rosie will keep what she knows to herself."

"Sort of the nature of the business, having to trust people who don't really deserve your trust. Except for you and me, everybody else is a criminal. Although you did steal this truck."

"You're an accessory. Which is why I now think you should come with me."

"I didn't even grab my toothbrush on the way out of my apartment."

"So, I'll buy you a new one." She paused. "I'm making you an offer here, Oscar, and I have to wonder why you're refusing it."

"Because I don't want to move. I don't want to spend the rest of my life looking over my shoulder. For you, it's worth it, because you're escaping from Gary."

"But he's going to be focused on you for helping me. Which makes me think the only reason you're not worried about that is you've made an arrangement."

"You come to me because you need my help. Then, because you need my help, you get all paranoid and sure I'll betray you."

"Convince me I'm wrong."

"Maybe you don't want me talking to Rosie alone, even though I'm the one she knows. Come in with me. Or go in yourself and say I sent you."

Liza weighed the options. "I'd rather do it together."

"Okay. We're good."

"If we were good, you'd come on the run with me."

"Liza Lee, I can't just pick up and go."

"That's what I'm doing. I didn't know I was stealing the truck until I stole it."

"You told me how much planning went into this."

"Whatever."

"I'm just not ready to leave my life behind, Chiquita."

"Fine." Liza continued looking ahead through the windshield, continued pushing the truck down the highway, the miles ticking away.

She sniffed. "This isn't what I wanted either, you know. To be on the run. I talk about Gary giving up after a while, but I'm just hoping that's what happens. Maybe he won't. Maybe Slick won't. Maybe I'll be looking over my shoulder for the rest of my life."

"Didn't you always?"

"When you put it that way."

"I mean, the money will help, certainly. It's a lot easier to hit the road with a bankroll, but you're going to have to settle down at some point, and that makes you discoverable."

"So, I should stop posting funny cat videos to social media with my address visible in the background?"

"You never posted cat videos." Oscar paused. "Did you?"

"Not likely."

"I get your point, though. You may never be free and clear. Maybe having me at your side would make you more visible, easier to describe."

"Yeah, there's that. You don't exactly blend in."

"If everybody else is already a shade of oil paint, I'm going to be a spray bottle of glitter."

"Not the best decision for someone in hiding."

Oscar's phone rang, and he answered it, "Ahoy!"

Maybe Liza hadn't woken him from a dream. Maybe he always answered the phone that way.

Oscar held out his device. "It's for you."

"For me?" Liza took the phone from him. "Hello?"

"I think you're in my truck."

Not Gary's voice. "Who is this?" Because maybe she was lucky, and this wasn't Slick.

"Word on the street, so I hear, is you're trying to find a buyer for my truck. Why would you be doing that?"

Liza rejected the first four responses that came to her. "I'm just following orders."

"Whose orders?"

"My boyfriend's."

"This boyfriend of yours have a name?"

"Gary. Gary Wilson."

She heard silence on the other end of the line.

A deep sigh. "What were his orders exactly?"

"He told me to take his truck and sell it by tomorrow."

"It's not his truck."

"Listen, I don't know who you are, but this truck has been sitting in his garage for almost two years now."

"It's still not his truck to sell."

"Maybe that's why he sent me to do it."

"Some people talk to Gary. You don't want to be there."

"Who is this?"

"You don't want to know that either."

"I just have to warn you. Gary is armed and dangerous. The only reason I agreed to do this was I knew he'd kill me if I didn't."

"You're not going to have to worry about Gary."

Liza swallowed. "I've heard that promise before."

"Not from me, you haven't."

"I don't even know who you are."

"How's my truck?"

"It's great. Seriously. Rides like a dream. I just filled the tank."

"You're going to bring it Huey's Auto Repair. One of my people will pick it up as soon as the shop opens."

Liza gripped the phone, wondering how far she could take this. "He promised me a cut."

"Huey?"

Better not make an enemy there, just in case she could ever use him in the future. "No, Gary. Gary said I could keep...twenty percent of whatever I got for the truck."

"Why would he offer you anything if he was your boyfriend, if you were scared of him?"

Good question, because he wouldn't. "Gary said he was giving me an incentive so I wouldn't get any bright ideas."

"Hmm."

"Besides, now I wouldn't have to borrow money from him for his birthday present."

"Don't worry. He won't be celebrating it."

"Maybe he had other reasons. I don't know. Gary's not exactly the most trustworthy person in the world. Sometimes he lies just so his other lies don't get lonely."

"Tell you what. You bring the truck to Huey's. If my person says the tank is full, if he says there's not a single scratch on the truck, I'll let you live."

"That's not exactly twenty percent."

"It's a good deal. It's the best deal you're going to get."

Liza licked her lips. A glass didn't need to contain much not to be empty. Anything less than completely empty was something.

If Slick got rid of Gary, she wouldn't even need the money to run.

She could make do going on as she had.

If Slick was still inside, calling her from an illegal phone, she was going to want Gary's body discovered before Slick was released.

She might be home free before she got home.

Liza continued driving one-handed. "Can I ask you a question?"

"Depends on the answer."

"I understand why you'd be mad at Gary, why you'd feel betrayed. I mean you trusted him to watch your truck, and then he turned around and sold it from under you."

"That's not a question."

"Can I count on you to protect your reputation?"

Silence.

Liza waited another beat. "I can't go home without the money from the sale. If I bring the truck to Huey's, and go home without Gary's money, I'm dead."

"It's not Gary's money."

"He thinks it is. He thinks he beat you."

"You don't have to worry about what Gary thinks or doesn't think."

Liza's breath caught, nearly causing her to choke. She swallowed several times in quick succession. "The truck will be at Huey's when the shop opens. Full tank. Not a scratch."

"Good."

Liza was listening to dead air. She passed the phone back to Oscar.

"What did you just do, Liza Lee?"

"I solved both of our problems."

"I understand that you're not Gary's biggest fan, but you probably just issued his death warrant."

"What if I did?"

Oscar did a double-take. "Is that really who you want to be? That's not half-empty or half-full. That's hurling the glass against the wall, and then using the broken pieces to cut somebody's face."

"You see any blood on my hands?"

Oscar shook his head. "Stealing a truck. It's just a thing."

"I've said it before, and I'll say it again. I can drop you off right here."

"Would you even slow down?"

Liza faced him. "Seriously? You're seriously going to ask me that?"

"Judging by your recent behavior, I'd say it's a valid question." Oscar glanced out his window. "We work together. We're work friends. How much do I really know about you?"

"I told Slick that selling the truck was Gary's idea. Would you rather I tell Slick it was yours?"

Oscar shook his head. "After we drop off the truck, that's it. We're done. I don't even know you anymore."

"Oscar—"

"What? Threatening to have me killed was just a joke? Don't I have a sense of humor? What's wrong with me?"

"We're tired. I'm tired. It's been a long, stressful night. In the morning, we'll dump the truck at Huey's, go somewhere for steak and eggs. We'll begin to feel better."

"Are you even pregnant?"

"I might be."

Oscar snorted. "So even that was lie."

"Not if I am. There's no reason to think I'm not."

"Is there any reason to think you are?"

Liza shrugged.

"Liza Lee, you're having Gary killed."

"It was him or us."

"No, you could have sold the truck and run. You chose to kill Gary instead."

"Slick would never have let us go. This way, we have a chance."

"I was helping my friend escape an abusive relationship."

"That's what you did."

"No. I watched my friend escape one monster only to become one herself."

Liza handed Huey the keys.

"I can have someone take you home."

She held up two fingers. "Give me a couple hours, please. I want to wait until I hear the news."

"What news?"

"I'll be out front."

Liza walked away from the truck and sat on the curb, wrapping her arms around her legs.

Turning her head to the right, she could see Oscar trudging down the sidewalk in the distance, his shoulders hunched, his hands in his pockets.

Her best friend in the whole wide world.

Then he turned a corner and disappeared.

HERE COMES THE JUDGE

James A. Hearn

Audra Skeletty was having the worst day of her life. She sat alone in a neatly appointed but dreary office in the Shady Rest Funeral Home, trying not to cry. The razor-thin silver lining to this dark cloud was that her father's final wishes would be honored, despite their eccentric nature and exorbitant expense, and the great Count Ivan Skeletty would finally be laid to rest. It had taken Audra three months and visits to dozens of Dallas-area funeral homes to find one willing to sell four adjoining plots for one person...and one unique coffin.

The director of the Shady Rest Funeral Home—a tall, spindly man with the unfortunate name of Barry Underhill—had stepped away to "attend to other customers." Since the adjoining offices were empty and no funerals were underway, Audra concluded these "customers" were dead; what their pressing needs might be, Underhill hadn't said. Perhaps it had something to do with the broken air conditioning system and the hundred-degree temperature outside.

Audra took a discreet sniff of her left underarm and frowned in disapproval. If the heat was causing her antiperspirant to fail, what effect would it have on unburied bodies, even embalmed ones? The morbid thought brought a fresh convulsion of blackened tears.

Dear God, why did I wear mascara and dark eyeshadow? Audra took a compact from her purse and flipped it open. In the mirror, gloomy smudges stared at her from a stranger's face. The furrows in her brow looked canyon-deep, her cheeks colorless and sunken save for rivulets of mascara. Her widow's peak of black hair, sharper and tinged with her first strands of gray, accentuated her skull. Since her father's passing from pancreatic cancer, she looked fifty instead of twenty-five.

"You're only as old as you feel," Audra said to the empty office. The echoing words broke the oppressive silence unique to morgues and graveyards that the living are loath to disturb. She shivered and said, "Too bad you feel like an old woman."

Once upon a time, her world was a fairy tale of promise and possibilities. Her father was a healthy, robust man who lived to perform as the self-titled Count Ivan Skeletty, Seer of All Things and Psychic to the Stars. They traveled from coast to coast in his beloved 1969 GTO The Judge convertible to sold-out shows; he astounded audiences with feats of mentalism, while Audra played the assistant and gifted daughter who'd inherited his psychic powers. Through sleight of hand, psychology, and careful observation of a volunteer, Count Skeletty could direct people to pick a specific card from a tarot deck or guess the contents of someone's pockets. For the masses, he wrote best-selling psychic self-help books; for the rich, he foretold the future and held séances to commune with their dead loved ones.

Fortune followed fame, and the demands for Count Skeletty grew shrill. With the passing years, the constant travel became an invisible weight on his shoulders. Her father was a motor at maximum throttle, living life at top-speed and continually pushing for the next public show or private session.

I'll retire soon, her father would say. For a man who sold lies for a living, it was the closest he'd come to lying to *her*.

Last Christmas, after a particularly grueling performance where he'd shamed yet another skeptic, he said over dinner, *I have my eye on a little Tuscan villa within walking distance of the Mar Ligure.*

Audra recalled hope swelling within her, a warm ocean wave threatening to sweep her away; sitting in the funeral home, the feeling was the dead memory of a stranger.

A Tuscan villa. Father, how splendid.

I'll tend an olive grove and drink too much wine; you'll marry some strapping local lad and bless me with grandchildren.

But the promised retirement to Tuscany never came. Out of the blue, a routine trip to the doctor for a recurring stomachache revealed inoperable cancer. In the space of three months, their dreams were laid aside as burdens, and her father's *joie de vivre* turned into a prayer for merciful death.

Audra snapped the compact shut so hard it cracked the mirror. It was hopeless; the more she dabbed at the runny mascara and eyeshadow with the morgue's lotion-infused Kleenex, the more it smeared, until the dark rings around her eyes rendered her as ghoulish as Underhill's other customers must look in this infernal, un-air-conditioned heat.

Outside, an engine growled to life and startled Audra into a nervous gasp. Beyond the window, she spied a backhoe tearing at the ground with a vengeance, preparing the earth to receive her father and his unusual coffin.

Do you jump at things that go bump in the night? Audra chided herself. *Are you the daughter of Count Ivan Skeletty, Seer of All Things and Psychic to the Stars? Or did he raise a slack-jawed rube who believes in ghosts?*

Her father believed in them, in the end. What a cosmically cruel joke that a skeptic and closeted atheist, a man who'd spent a lifetime convincing the gullible he communicated with spirits, would have a deathbed conversion.

In his final days, the kind, gentle George Herbert Johnson from Tulsa, Oklahoma—known the world over as Count Ivan Skeletty—lost his mind, and his ramblings in the wee hours before dawn became unbearable.

Josephine. Josephine, my darling.

There was his wife and the mother Audra had never known,

sitting in the blue velvet rocking chair where she'd hoped to nurse Audra.

Calloway. I tried to save you, but the water was cold, so cold. Dear brother, forgive me.

Over there, the long-dead brother who'd slipped beneath the ice of a winter lake at the tender age of eight; by the door, the irascible Uncle Skinner, the original owner of the GTO convertible; flying overhead, Granddaddy Paul Johnson, a decorated aviator who'd twice escaped from German POW camps; and a parade of names Audra didn't know, from times long past.

During these nightly visions, Audra held her father's hand and wondered if the cancer had taken root in his brain. Were his synapses so tangled that he believed the dead were with him, all the time, everywhere, waiting sadly—or eagerly—for the living to join them?

Sitting in the funeral parlor, Audra herself wasn't sure what to believe. All she knew was that George Herbert Johnson had left her an orphan, albeit a rich one, and life in general was a shadowy reflection of its former vibrant self.

Audra looked down at the tarot cards in her hands. How long had she been holding them? She hadn't been aware of taking them out of her purse or shuffling them on the desk of the absentee undertaker.

The tarot cards were well-worn, an early Rider—Waite edition from 1919; this was her father's go-to deck when he wanted to perform a "controlled" reading for a desired outcome. Any half-skilled hack with a neon sign and some incense could interpret the cards to provide clients with the answers they desired; but it was so much easier to use a marked deck to predict the future.

Trouble with love? *What's this, the Lovers, and in the correct orientation to boot. How lucky.* Financial woes? *Look, a reversed Wheel of Fortune. Better days are coming, my friend, by and by.*

Audra didn't believe in the tarot any more than she believed in Santa Claus, but she did find the gentle sliding of the cards between her fingers oddly soothing. Without looking at them, she laid a card on the table to represent the past.

Audra saw the Magician, the first numbered card of the Major Arcana, staring at her with his inscrutable gaze. His right hand held a double-ended white wand and was pointing towards the sky, while the left pointed to the earth: a bridge between the spiritual and physical planes of reality, as her father explained in his books. On a nearby table rested the four suits of the Minor Arcana: sword, cup, pentacle, and wand.

Well, that's too easy. It didn't take a psychic to see the Magician was George Herbert Johnson, aka Count Skeletty, and he lived in the past.

Audra laid down the next card, selected at random, to represent the present. The Chariot, upside down. The Major Arcana's seventh card was a regal charioteer carrying a wand, as did the Magician. Two sphinxes pulled the chariot without reins, guided solely by the stars above the charioteer's crowned head.

Audra had always admired this card; its symmetry was aesthetically pleasing, its imagery powerful. But in reversed position, the Chariot represented conflict, quarrel, riot, litigation, dispute, and defeat. In her present circumstances, the meaning was much more literal: the Chariot was her father's GTO convertible, parked outside, and the reversed position was a manifestation of her father's eccentric final wishes.

For the first time in weeks, Audra almost laughed. If she didn't know better, she'd swear the spirits were playing a joke with these prescient cards. What was next? Death, to represent her father's funeral?

It was time to see the future. Again, without looking at the marked deck, she pulled a third and final card. This time, not one, but two cards fell to the table. Two diverging futures then, or perhaps a future path incorporating both cards?

The first card was the Tower, the sixteenth trump of the Major Arcana. Although the card could have positive implications, the Count rarely dealt it for the future position, unless he wanted to prevent someone from pursuing a dangerous goal. The image of lightning striking the tower's top, coupled with the man and woman plunging to their deaths, represented unforeseen catastrophe. The only cards more feared in the entire tarot were Death and the Devil.

Thankfully, the second card representing her possible future was neither Death nor the Devil, but she didn't like it much better. Audra tapped the Fool with the tip of a red lacquered nail. Was she the young man on the card, so blithely walking toward the edge of a cliff, a white dog dancing at his heels? In carrying out her father's final wishes, she certainly felt a fool. Or were there other players coming into her life, their lines as-yet unwritten, fools marching toward the disaster represented by the Tower?

From somewhere in the building, an air conditioning unit kicked on with an audible whoosh. A few moments later, Underhill returned to the office, a whiff of formaldehyde clinging to his clothes. He took a seat behind his desk, opened a drawer, and took out a file marked COUNT IVAN SKELETTY. When he saw her smeared makeup, he gave a start but quickly recovered himself.

"My apologies, Mrs. Skeletty. The HVAC service has completed repairs on our units. In these sweltering summers, you can't imagine the havoc unconditioned air can wreck in my line of work."

"It's Ms. Skeletty. Ivan Skeletty was my father; I never knew my mother."

"Never knew your mother?"

Audra scooped up the tarot cards and returned them to her purse. "She died in childbirth."

"Ah yes, so it says in the obituary." Underhill scanned the file, his fingers stroking his pointed chin. "I see you have not one but *four* plots for your father." He glanced out the window to the industrious backhoe. "Most unusual. Yes, most unusual."

"Count Ivan Skeletty was an unusual man."

Underhill put down the file, the upturned corners of his mouth revealing pearly teeth beneath colorless lips. "Indeed. I read his memoirs, *Crossing the Great Unknown*. He was so..."

"Insightful?" Audra offered.

"Exactly. He had The Gift"—the capital letters were clear in Underhill's words—"if anyone did. Of course, on my humble pay, I could never afford a reading with anyone close to your father's talents, or yours. Pardon me for not recognizing you earlier. Kleenex?"

Audra waved the box away. "No thank you, Mr. Underhill. You'd think that a psychic would've foreseen that mascara was a bad choice for today."

"Tut tut, Ms. Skeletty. You're here, fulfilling a daughter's duty. That's more than may be said for many. Some can't afford to bury their dead, so they simply leave them where they are, to rot, until someone calls the authorities and the taxpayers foot the bill."

Audra took out her checkbook and said, "If there's nothing else, I believe the balance is due on the account?"

Underhill rambled for some minutes, not sensing that Audra was eager to be away. The obituary she'd written was a marvelous tribute to her father and would be published online tonight. Yes, his final wishes were a tad strange, but then, who could judge such matters? No, she wasn't up to giving a reading, at present. Would another day do as well?

Audra was rising from her chair when a familiar sound arrested her attention. The backhoe outside was still digging a hole four plots wide, but that wasn't what filled her with fear. This new sound was a powerful but smaller engine, more of a throaty purr than a growl.

The GTO. Audra sprang to the window to see a man in a Dallas Cowboys jersey getting into her father's car. The engine was running; had she left the keys in the ignition for this thief?

"What's the matter?" Underhill asked.

Audra didn't answer. Snatching up her purse, she ran outside in time to see the GTO pulling away from the curb.

"Stop! Stop, thief!" As she fumbled for the phone in her purse, Audra locked eyes with the man in the GTO. In that brief moment, she memorized his every feature. He had a kind face for a would-be thief, deeply dimpled cheeks framing a narrow nose, and she had the impression his head was shaved under his ball cap. But what struck her most was the wide-eyed look of sheer panic.

He's scared of me, Audra realized. Was it her smudged makeup and the sweat-soaked hair plastered to her scalp that made him think she was a cadaver come to life?

No matter; Audra's questing fingers found her phone, and she began lifting it out. Instead of driving away as he should, the man in the GTO was reaching for something, too. It wasn't a gun—a thought that raced through her mind without frightening her— but some strange amulet he'd hung from the rearview mirror. In the sunlight, it flickered with a demonic flame, a crazy collection of golden luck charms.

With the amulet in his one hand, the man pointed to her and cried, "Back to the depths, you undead freak!" as another man's voice said, "Drive, you moron!"

Seemingly on cue, the heel of Audra's left shoe landed between two concrete pavers and broke off. Audra stumbled, her phone and purse slipping from her grasp as if tugged by unseen hands. Her father's tarot cards fluttered all around her, some dancing away in a hot breeze that sprang out of nowhere before dying as quickly as it had come.

By the time she had the 9-1-1 operator on the line, the GTO was tearing out of the parking lot, followed closely by a blond man driving a white SUV. This new culprit looked of an age with the first man, likely mid-twenties. Whereas the thief was lean, his partner—he must've been the man who yelled for the "moron" to drive away—was thick through the shoulders, his blue eyes grim as he passed.

In seconds, the two vehicles were gone, leaving Audra alone on the hot pavement outside the Shady Rest Funeral Home.

Although she'd committed their features to memory, she hadn't caught the SUV's license plate. Unfortunately, she'd never been good at picking out the makes and models of vehicles and couldn't tell the 9-1-1 operator what the second man was driving. But what should that matter? Since there were only one hundred and eight 1969 GTO The Judge convertibles in existence, the unique car should be easy for the police to find.

Meanwhile, Underhill appeared and was apologizing profusely for the theft. "The unmitigated gall, Ms. Skeletty. In thirty years, no one has stolen so much as a paperclip from here."

"It's a brave new world, Mr. Underhill. Raging pandemics, runaway inflation, political upheavals, and desperate people."

"Wars and rumors of wars," Underhill groaned. He started picking up her tarot cards, counting to himself as he thumbed through them. "Seventy-six. You're missing two cards, I'm afraid." He paused and said solemnly, "Given your father's final wishes, how would you care to proceed?"

Care to proceed? She'd start by strangling the two Fools who'd stolen the Magician's Chariot and finish by flinging their bodies from the top of the Tower. Then the import of Underhill's words registered in her mind.

"Missing two cards?" Audra asked. "Which two?"

Underhill flicked through the tarot deck again. "The Tower and the Fool."

Audra took the remaining cards from the undertaker; they were icy cold to the touch. Was it coincidence that the cards representing her future were missing? Where were they? Her mind replayed an image of the thief grabbing his luck charms, the heel of her shoe breaking, and the contents of her purse flying into the air. A strange, unexpected breeze had carried some of the cards towards the convertible...

With Underhill, Audra did a quick search of the sidewalk and the parking lot, but their efforts proved what she already knew. The two cards were not here.

Underhill coughed into his hand. "Ms. Skeletty? Shall we at

least cancel the obituary?"

Audra's voice was murderous. "Run the obituary, Mr. Underhill; with a few alterations, it may help me catch a couple of Fools."

Earlier that day, Brad Connolly was riding shotgun in a stolen Lexus LX 600 SUV with his brother, Rolly Rojas. The men weren't really brothers, though they introduced themselves as such. In fact, the two orphans were as different as men could be in appearance and attitudes; but like family related by blood, they sometimes drove each other nuts.

"Rolly, only a fool believes in ghosts," Brad said from the passenger's seat. To emphasize the point, Brad slapped the console dividing the front seats too forcefully, tossing a plastic cup of sunflower seeds into the air.

As seeds scattered everywhere, Rolly flinched like a coulrophobic kid when a clown pops out of a jack-in-the-box. As he involuntarily jerked the steering wheel to the left, the stolen SUV's wheels veered across the double yellow line of a two-lane Texas highway.

In the opposite lane, an eighteen-wheeler crested a hill, the engine whispering the promise of fiery death across the rapidly narrowing distance. With a yell, Brad reached across the console and tugged the steering wheel to the right. The Lexus lurched into the proper lane, and the big rig's horn bellowed as the behemoth passed them by.

As fate receded into the rearview mirror, Rolly let loose a string of profanities in two languages. He coughed out the last of the sunflower seeds he'd nearly swallowed and cried, "Brad, are you trying to make us into ghosts? I swear to God, I will haunt your ass if you get us killed."

"If *I* get us killed?" Brad said, a vein throbbing in his left temple with each word and his freckled face a shade paler. "*You're* driving."

"I didn't throw seeds into the air."

Brad shook his shaggy head of blond hair. "You overreact when there's trouble; it's a good thing you have me around."

"I'd still haunt your ass, out of spite," Rolly muttered.

"How can you haunt me if we're both dead?" Brad asked in exasperation. "But no one is haunting anyone, because—"

"Don't say it," Rolly interjected. "You'll make them angry." Steering with his knees, he began gathering up sunflower seeds and putting them back into his cup. *Waste not, want not.* It was a painful lesson they'd learned in the Saint Jerome Orphanage in San Antonio.

"Ghosts aren't real," Brad finished in a huff. He whistled, a discordant pitch that modulated from low to high, landed in between, then trailed off ominously. "Spirits, this is Bradley David Connolly of Dallas, Texas. I'm an orphan, a car thief, and I deny your existence. In fact, I dare you to strike me down."

Rolly cringed with every word, but nothing happened. No unseen spirits cried out in anger, no pockets of cold air descended to flood them with inexplicable dread. The stolen Lexus continued peacefully down the highway toward Huey's Auto Repair, where it would be dismantled for spare parts.

Brad breathed easier. "The universe is similar to this Lexus. It's an extremely complex—"

Rolly held up a hand and said, "No way. If anything, the universe would be something much cooler than a Lexus. How about a 1955 Mercedes-Benz 300 SLR Uhlenhaut Coupe? That's the most expensive car in the world."

"I was speaking metaphorically," Brad said.

Rolly shrugged. "Sure, but let's agree the universe is at least a Mercedes."

"Fine. The universe is a Mercedes, an extremely complex mechanism governed by physical laws. From the largest galaxy down to the subatomic quark, there is no *super*natural, only the natural."

"Don't you believe in God, even a little?" Rolly asked.

"A wise man proportions his belief to the evidence. Since I don't have any evidence for God, at least none that would pass scientific muster, my level of belief is zero."

Rolly's long exhalation whistled out of his narrow nose. "That's an empty life. A person has to believe in something beyond *this*." He thumped the 4 on his Dak Prescott Dallas Cowboys jersey. "Something that gives life meaning."

Brad patted the dashboard of the stolen Lexus. "I believe in a dishonest day's pay for a dishonest day's work. Now, if you can get us to Huey's without killing us..."

"We'll get to Huey's in one piece if you don't throw seeds at me."

Brad let the argument drop. His thoughts turned to tonight's revels, after Huey paid them. Flush with cash, they'd pick up pizzas from Little Nero's, get smashed on whiskey sours, and play World of Warcraft. When they were good and lit, they'd finish the night at the Jolly Irishman Pub down the street from their apartment. Darts, cheap beer, some tipsy SMU co-eds slumming it with two local boys, and the typical Friday night would come to a typical end.

Brad settled into his seat with visions of pizza and bubbly co-eds dancing in his head, but this didn't cheer him as it usually did. It was a sobering thought to realize the universe—that uncaring operation of physical laws he had praised a few minutes ago—was continuing on its merry way, a Mercedes-Benz driving down a highway not caring that a big rig had almost transformed the Lexus into a toaster and them into human Pop-Tarts.

"So, in the world according to Brad, when you're dead, what's next?" Rolly asked.

"You're D-E-A-D," Brad spelled the word letter by letter, "as the proverbial doornail. And you stay dead for the rest of forever, in an unbearable silence of loneliness until everything, every-where, assumed a temperature of absolute zero."

"That's cold-blooded," Rolly said.

Brad agreed that it was. *In the heat death of the universe, entropy was the Conqueror Worm.* He'd written that in his journal late one night, puzzling over the end of himself and the end of everything. He'd also been quite drunk.

"It's all over in one googol years," Brad muttered.

"One Google years?"

"One *googol* years. That's 10 to the 100th power years."

"What's over?" Rolly asked.

Brad spread his hands. "Everything."

Rolly groaned. "Amigo, two semesters of junior college do not make you Neil deGas Tyson."

"Neil deGrasse Tyson," Brad corrected. "He doesn't believe in superstitions and neither do I."

Rolly's scowl deepened. "That astronomy asshole is on my shit list. He killed my favorite planet because it's *too little*. Dwarf planets, eh? That's racist, man. We should be calling them little-person planets."

"Are you mental?"

"You heard me," Rolly said. "It's not enough that we're screwing up the Earth; we're extending bad karma into space."

Brad threw up his hands. "Karma? The universe plays by its own rules, Rolly. It doesn't care about the little four-leaf clovers on that ridiculous amulet you're wearing." At this remark, Rolly's hand flew to his heart where his crazy collection of luck charms lay. "My friend, you're nothing but a walking, talking assembly of biochemical reactions with the illusion of freewill." Another golden nugget scribbled in his journal after too much Crown Royal Vanilla.

Without warning, Rolly reached over and rapped his knuckles on Brad's blockish blond head.

"Ow! What did you do that for?"

"My freewill said to," Rolly answered. "That's for Pluto, and your oversized Irish noggin is the closest thing to wood in this SUV. I ain't taking any more chances today. Not on today, of all days."

"It's Friday. So what?"

Rolly lapsed into a truculent silence. He stared straight ahead, both hands firmly on the steering wheel. He was more than a little agitated, Brad realized. The man was truly scared about something, and not from their mutual near-death experience. What was it?

Brad's blue eyes lit with understanding. *Today, of all days. Holy shit, it's Friday the thirteenth.* No wonder the poor bastard was on edge; Rolly probably expected a maniac in a hockey mask to leap out of every shadow, machete raised for a killing blow.

As if hedging his bets against such an eventuality, Rolly pulled his lucky amulet from beneath his jersey, kissed it, and hung the gaudy thing from the rearview mirror. The various golden charms were an odd assortment of cultural appropriations: four leaf clovers, knots, dreamcatchers, an ankh, and other symbols Brad couldn't identify. With all that gold, it looked like a Mr. T starter kit for the extremely superstitious.

Brad opened his mouth, then closed it again. What was the point? Rolly had always been this way, even back in the orphanage they'd aged out of because nobody wanted them. The poor kid received twice the punishments as Brad, since Sister Maria did not tolerate Rolly's unorthodox views that there were more things in heaven and earth than were dreamt of in the nun's philosophy. A holy Trinity? *Of course*, declared Sister Maria. Angels? *A million of them could dance on the head of a pin.* Demons? *A third of the angels joined with Lucifer.* But Rolly's ghosts were dismissed as superstitious nonsense, a substitute religion that ensnared the feebleminded.

Rolly wasn't persuaded by Sister Maria's dogma nor dissuaded by her ruler. Even today, at age twenty-seven, black cats and broken mirrors would send him running for the hills, if the city had hills, to avoid bad luck.

Through the years, Brad had tried his best to ignore his best friend's irrational fears and unconventional beliefs. After all, Rolly was the closest thing to family he'd ever known, and was there anything more important to an orphan than family? *Someone* had to take care of the crazy guy, and, by the God that Brad refused to believe in, that someone was him.

Maybe one day, when Brad earned enough dough boosting cars for Huey, he'd go back to school and become a psychiatrist. In these visions, his first patient would be the incurably superstitious Rolly Rojas who believed *Poltergeist* and *The Amityville Horror* were documentaries.

"There *are* ghosts whether you believe in them or not," Rolly said, as if reading Brad's thoughts.

"Shut up and drive."

But Rolly did not shut up and drive; if he was awake, he was talking. And if he was talking, it was usually about subjects Brad cared nothing about. If it wasn't about his precious Cowboys, it was about ghosts, government conspiracies, UFOs, vampires, cryptids, or videos from the deepest, darkest corners of the internet. Big-headed and bug-eyed aliens with pale skin built the pyramids, secret societies of vampires prowled the world's cities, and Bigfoot was out there somewhere, the all-time champion of hide-and-seek.

But none of these reality-warping mysteries inspired Rolly with such fascination—and outright dread—the way ghosts did. According to Rolly, the dearly departed were everywhere, all the time, even in the backseat of this stolen Lexus they'd boosted from a country club.

"And these ghosts are perpetually pissed," Rolly finished. He drummed his long fingers nervously on the steering wheel, his dark eyes flicking to the back seat. He pulled at his Dak Prescott jersey and said, "Is it hot in here to you? Like, *unnaturally* hot."

Brad mopped his square chin with a T-shirt that said, *Pi is better than cake.* "Of course it's hot in here. The A/C for this stupid Lexus you picked out doesn't work, it's Texas in the summertime, and climate change is changing the planet into a poached egg."

"I don't believe in that global warming crap," Rolly said. "It's all a scam to make Al Gore money."

Brad pinched the bridge of his nose, took a calming breath, and refused to be baited into another of Rolly's anti-science conspiracy theories. When he felt his blood pressure approaching normal levels, Brad embraced the madness and said, "I thought ghosts were supposed to be *cold*, not hot."

"Normally, that's true," Rolly said. He turned into a Whataburger parking lot and pulled into line for the drive-thru. "The average ghost will create a cold spot, a temperature differential. But angry ghosts, or ghosts that've been to hell, can heat up a room in moments. It's on that YouTube video I sent yesterday."

Brad fished his wallet from a jeans pocket. "Deleted, my friend. Get me a number three with a large Coke. That's convenient about the temperatures, don't you think?"

"What's convenient?" Rolly asked after placing their orders.

"That these supposed ghost hunters"—here Brad inserted air quotes—"can use their bogus gadgets and claim areas of low temperature or hot temperature are evidence of paranormal activity. I mean, anywhere you go there'll be areas hotter or colder than normal."

Rolly took off his ball cap and scratched his head; the glistening sweat on his shaved scalp formed a halo, giving him an angelic appearance that would've made Sister Maria cross herself. "Huh. And I guess it's okay for your so-called global warming that scientists claim totally contradictory things as evidence?"

"Contradictory?" Brad repeated.

"You heard me," Rolly said. "Having a drought? Blame global warming. Too much rain? Also global warming. Oceanic currents are slowing down or speeding up, hurricanes are weaker or stronger...all global warming. And who's getting richer? The politicians and the companies they invest in."

"How can you ignore the evidence?"

"Evidence?" Rolly scoffed. "They cook the books on that stuff more than an Enron accountant."

The drive-thru attendant handed Rolly their dinner and the Lexus once again took to the road. Brad unwrapped Rolly's burger, placed his partner-in-crime's fries and beverage in the cup holders, and then attacked a bacon cheeseburger.

With a burger in one hand and the other on the steering wheel, Rolly fell silent. He even waved to a cop who let them merge onto the highway, and they drove in silence for several miles.

Brad chewed meditatively, knowing he should be enjoying the rare peace. But he could never leave well enough alone. His burger and fries finished, he sipped his Coke and took up their long-standing argument. "And what *evidence* do you have for ghosts? Have you seen one?" Brad asked this with the confidence of a man who already knows the answer is no.

"Yes, I have," Rolly said with a faraway look.

In the dead silence, Brad choked on the ice he was chewing. He coughed it back into the Styrofoam cup and said, "Bullshit."

"Have I ever lied to you, Brad?"

Before he could answer, Brad's phone buzzed with an incoming text. He read the message, scowling.

"Who is it?" Rolly asked.

Brad cleared his throat, then schooled his features to stillness before answering. "No big deal. It's a text from one of Huey's spotters. He has a hot lead on a vintage GTO, a rush job that has to be boosted right away."

"Now? But we have a car all ready to go; our work is done for the day."

"When Huey says jump, do we stop and ask how high? No; we jump. Besides, there's nobody faster than you on a GTO, am I right?"

"True Dak," Rolly said.

Brad pointed his index finger into his mouth and made a gagging motion. "Stop that. No one is going to start saying, *True Dak* instead of *True dat*. And no one but aging hipsters are saying that these days."

"Cowboys fans will say *True Dak*," Rolly said. "Look, it's going to catch on when we win the Super Bowl, so you might as well get onboard the bandwagon for America's Team. Plenty of room." Rolly rubbed his dexterous hands together gleefully. "A rush job for Huey means more money. This will definitely get us back into his good graces, amigo."

"Let's hope so," Brad said quietly. Only two people had ever inspired the Irish car thief with genuine fear. One was Father Flanagan, a reed-thin priest at the orphanage with a voice that could curdle milk. The other was the mysterious sole proprietor of Huey's Auto Repair.

The big man was lavish with rewards for his top earners, and equally lavish with punishment for those who displeased him. Or so the stories went. One unfortunate thief named Keith had apparently brought in a BMW whose former owner was the wife of a local police captain. No one knew exactly what happened to Keith...but the next day Huey's office had new carpet, patched drywall, fresh paint, and the unmistakable odor of bleach.

Rolly was blithely talking about the money they'd make, oblivious to his friend's dark thoughts. "Tell me where this GTO is, and I'll bag it so quick your head will spin faster than Linda Blair's in *The Exorcist*. True story, by the way."

"No, it's best you stay on a need-to-know basis until we get there," Brad said cryptically. "Turn left at the next light."

Rolly spun the wheel. "Need to know? I'm driving; I have to know, or how am I going to get there?"

"You're not going to like it, Rolly."

When they arrived at their destination, Rolly didn't like it one damn bit.

"I don't like it," Rolly said. He drummed his fingers on the Lexus's steering wheel in obvious apprehension. The SUV idled beneath a canopy of ancient live oaks near the entrance to the Shady Rest

Funeral Home. They were on the outskirts of a quiet suburban neighborhood, and the summer sun was sinking behind a bank of bloody clouds that hugged the horizon.

"What's wrong with the setup?" Brad asked.

Rolly didn't want to say. He'd never cared for cemeteries, even in broad daylight, and he avoided funerals at all costs. Not that *every* cemetery was haunted; just most of them.

Brad, in his logical, Mr. Spock voice, was pointing out that the parking lot was nearly empty, save for an HVAC repair van and the GTO convertible sitting all by its lonesome. The car's top was down, an open invitation for someone with the proper skills to drive it away. Traffic was light, the funeral home had no security cameras, and their portable police scanner indicated no activity in the neighborhood. In less than sixty seconds, one of them could be behind the GTO's wheel and on the way to Huey's.

"Easy peasy, nice and cheesy," Brad said.

Too easy, Rolly thought. The one weird thing was the backhoe, beyond the cemetery's wrought-iron gate, digging a hole big enough to bury an elephant. He'd read about some guy in Illinois who'd weighed over a thousand pounds and had to be buried in a piano case.

"What's up with the backhoe?" Brad asked, abstracted with the same thought.

"Dunno. Did morbidly obese Siamese twins die?"

"We don't say *Siamese* twins anymore, Rolly."

"How come?"

Brad rolled his eyes. "It's offensive. We say *conjoined* twins."

"Pardon me, Ms. Manners. If you can say dwarf planet, I can say Siamese twins."

"Back to our GTO," Brad said. "Is there something wrong you're seeing that I'm not?"

"There's nothing wrong with the setup," Rolly admitted.

"Then what?"

Rolly massaged his temples to coax the words from his brain. He didn't want to admit this place gave him the creeps, so he tried a different tactic. "You talk a good game about our words, correcting me whenever I say something remotely offensive. But you don't live it, Brad."

"Don't beat around the bush. Tell me why I'm such a terrible person."

"We're living in a society, and we're supposed to act in a civilized way. I ask you, is it civilized to steal from someone who may be grieving?"

"Nice try, Rolly. But you'll have to do better than quoting George Costanza to talk your way out of this job. I was sitting on the same couch, eating the same nachos, and smoking the same weed when 'The Chinese Restaurant' episode came on."

"They're George's words, but they were truth," Rolly said. "*We're living in a society,* and stealing this car from a funeral home is a huge violation of karmic principle."

Brad didn't bother to hide the exasperation in his voice. "We don't have principles, karmic or otherwise. We're car thieves. We don't steal from the rich and give to the poor; we steal from everyone. Speaking of stealing, take a gander at that convertible, my friend."

Reluctantly, Rolly lifted his head and looked.

"Don't you want to drive it, even if it's for a few minutes?"

Rolly stared at the GTO, his lips curving upward. The car sparkled, a giant orange diamond in the dying sunlight. Even at this distance, it was obvious the owner had meticulously cared for this car, preserving it against the ravages of time.

Brad, scrolling through his phone, gave a low whistle. "The Google machine says one hundred and eight GTO Judges left the assembly lines without a roof, as convertibles. This car would sell for half a million dollars, easy. And *you* could drive it."

"I could drive it," Rolly repeated dreamily. He had the glazed look of an alcoholic anticipating the first sip of a weekend bender. He gathered himself and said, "I'm a thief; guilty as charged. There's The Judge waiting over there to convict me. But let's talk this out. What if some poor soul is inside that funeral home as we speak, making final arrangements for a loved one? They're having the worst day ever, and what do they find when they come outside? Their vintage GTO, stolen."

"We don't have a choice," Brad said. "Huey would have our heads if he missed out on this $500,000 prize because you grew a conscience."

At the mention of money, Rolly's karmic misgivings melted away and were replaced by a more earthly thought. "Hold on, did you say that car is worth half a million dollars?"

"I've said that. Twice."

"What if we, you know..." Rolly's voice died away, unable to articulate the dangerous thought.

"Know what?"

"We say we missed it."

Brad's brow furrowed thoughtfully. "When we pulled up, we tell Huey there was no GTO, is that it?"

"Exactly, amigo. We steal it for ourselves."

Brad slapped Rolly's forehead with a palm and said, "You need a brain transplant."

Rolly rubbed his head. "I may be bald and you have a bad haircut, but I'm not Curly to your Mo."

"Then don't be a stooge who says things that could get us killed."

"Okay, crossing Huey is a dumb idea. But I'm not taking on bad karma to make some other schmuck rich. You can be part of that story, not me."

"Here's a story I don't want to be a part of," Brad said. "I don't want to be the one to tell Huey how we lost this specially requested GTO because we were dicking around in the parking lot. You want to talk about bad karma? Huey will give you all the bad karma you could ever want, firsthand. Remember Keith?"

Rolly swallowed hard, his Adam's apple bobbing up and down in his throat. Convinced of the point, he put his lucky amulet back on and grabbed a length of wire and a screwdriver from his stash of tools in the backseat. He shoved the screwdriver into his pocket, opened the SUV's door, and said, "See you at Huey's."

"I'd wish you good luck, if I believed in it."

"Do it anyway."

Brad did not wish him luck. Instead, he talked about what they'd do with their money. He suggested taking a weekend trip to San Antonio to cruise the old stomping grounds, reliving their first night of freedom from the orphanage when'd they'd boosted a Cadillac and got loaded like freight trains. "What do you say, Rolly? We could have a weekend bender in San Antonio. I promise, tomorrow night we'll be toasting Mexican martinis on the River—"

But Rolly closed the door, not hearing the rest of Brad's promise. He turned to the GTO parked near the funeral home's entrance. It was a gorgeous car, sleek yet powerful, a fortune on four wheels. And he would have the honor of driving it. On the way to Huey's, he'd pretend it was his; he'd take the long way to the chop shop, savoring every moment behind the wheel. He could picture Brad riding behind in the Lexus, cursing him for the unnecessary risk.

Rolly cracked his knuckles. *Well, this GTO isn't going to steal itself.* He strode purposefully toward the car, wire under his jersey and screwdriver in his pocket. In seconds, the hood was up and he was looking down at a spotlessly clean engine. That in itself was a thing of beauty, the hallmark of a devoted owner.

Rolly connected the hotwire between the positive on the battery and the positive on the coil, then took out his screwdriver. On these older Pontiacs, the starter relay was built into the solenoid and positioned underneath the car, but that was no problem when you had a long enough screwdriver and knew the precise angle to stick it...

The engine started.

Easy peasy, nice and cheesy. Exactly as Brad had said, the bastard. They'd deliver their prizes to Huey, get paid, and celebrate in San Antonio. But once there, Rolly planned to do more than party; he was going to prove to his friend, once and for all, that ghosts *were real*. There was no better place than San Antonio's haunted railroad crossing, near the intersection of Villamain and Shane, where legend says a school bus full of kids stalled on the tracks, may God rest their souls.

Rolly crossed himself and hopped into the GTO. The seat was warm from the sunlight, yet comfortable, but the steering wheel was too hot to touch. He blew into his palms and grabbed it again, this time not letting go. How funny that the most enjoyable things in life always came with a built-in price, paid in money or exacted as pain.

Sighing, Rolly took his lucky amulet from around his neck and hung it from the rearview mirror. It had cost a fortune and an incredible amount of internet research to assemble the ultimate good luck charm, but it was worth every penny. It had saved their lives earlier today when that big rig had missed them by a black cat's whisker, that was certain, and the amulet would see him safely to Huey's.

Rolly was pulling away from the curb when the doors to the funeral home flew open. Someone—*or was it something?*—was running toward the GTO with a wordless snarl. Ghost or reanimated cadaver, Rolly wasn't sure which, but it was female, raven hair plastered to her skull and dark smudges where her eyes should be.

The thing screamed, "Stop! Stop, thief!"

Instinctively, Rolly reached for the golden charm hanging from the rearview mirror and cried, "Back to the depths, you undead freak!"

At that moment, the purse in her hands seemed to burst apart, giant playing cards scattering in a sudden breeze. Two of the cards flew toward him like giant moths, and he swatted the things away from his face.

Another voice screamed, "Drive, you moron!"

Rolly obeyed Brad's command; he floored the accelerator and sped away from the funeral home, followed by Brad in the Lexus.

It was some minutes before it occurred to Rolly that the undead didn't carry purses and cell phones. *Probably not, anyway.* He continued to Huey's, unaware of two tarot cards stirring fitfully under his seat.

It was obvious to Rolly that Huey's Auto Repair was haunted. He felt chills every time they brought in a stolen car, even in the dog days of a Texas summer, when triple digit temperatures could kill you.

And if Huey's wasn't haunted, it was definitely cursed. Was there any stronger prayer than a dying man's against his killer, even though the prayer be evil? Did Keith's shade brood beside the thieves and stare baleful daggers at his former employer?

Huey himself was oblivious to the darkness pervading his business. The big man was standing casually by the GTO without a care in the world. "What a remarkable piece of engineering and design. When the spotter informed me he had tapped you two for this job, I had my doubts. But here you are, with a 1969 Pontiac GTO The Judge convertible in immaculate condition. Why, even the trinkets hanging from the rearview mirror are extraordinary."

It was after hours at Huey's, and with the service bay doors securely closed, the big man's baritone voice echoed off the walls and came back to Rolly's ears as dying whispers. The car thief tried to hide his discomfiture behind his usual easy manner, but his stomach churned with acid whenever he talked with the owner of the illegal chop shop hidden within a legitimate auto repair business.

Huey was about sixty years old, Rolly guessed, but there was nothing particularly warm or grandfatherly about him. Dressed in his crisp black suit, he radiated a quiet menace, an undertaker in search of a customer.

The repair shop was a reflection of its owner, as spotless as Huey's custom-made suit. No grease stains marred the floors, the rafters were free of cobwebs, and the toilets in the men's room were pristine. There wasn't even a misplaced wrench at Huey's; it was unnatural for a garage to be so incredibly clean, and it added to Rolly's heebie-jeebies.

If Brad felt any discomfort, the Irishman gave no sign. He was talking too much and too fast, as he always did around Huey. He was bound to say something stupid, and soon, if he went on much longer. They should get their money and blow town.

"You should've seen Rolly in action, Huey," Brad was saying. "So smooth, so fast. Quick as lightning, we left the funeral home in the rearview mirror."

Brad was conveniently leaving out the part about the ghastly woman who'd run after them, a screaming banshee come to life. It was just as well, as Rolly didn't want to think about her any more than necessary. Those black eyes would be haunting his dreams for years to come, he was sure.

"Funeral home?" A Black man in his early fifties raised his head up from behind the GTO. He paused his efforts to open the trunk with a locksmith kit, his lips pursed in a sardonic smile. "You snatched this baby from a *funeral home*?"

"That's correct, Rashad," Brad said. "The Shady Rest Funeral Home. Big trees. Looked nice and quiet, except for a backhoe digging a grave for some fat guy."

Rashad's eyes narrowed, his taut skin enhancing the zig-zag scar on his left cheek. "You wouldn't find me stealing a car from a funeral home. Bad karma."

Rolly thought Huey's stony countenance almost cracked into a grin, but the big man's facial muscles seemed unused to such an exertion, and he merely chuckled under his breath.

"Bad karma?" Huey said. "Rashad, you are the best mechanic in the business. When we service vehicles for police officers, you have nerves of steel and never bat an eye. I had no idea you were so squeamish."

Rashad returned his attention to the still-locked trunk. "Boss, there's bad karma out there. And it could get stuck to the bottom of your shoes."

"Amen," Rolly said a bit too loudly.

Brad glared at him. "Don't mind my partner, Huey. He's had a long—"

Huey held up a hand, palm facing Brad's mouth, and the thief's teeth clicked shut. "Explain yourself, Roland."

Roland. Only Huey and Sister Maria had ever called him that. It put him at a disadvantage, reduced him to being a kid again. Nevertheless, Rolly squared his shoulders and said, "The spirit world keeps a tally of what we do."

"A ledger of our deeds," Rashad's disembodied voice said from behind the GTO. It was hard to get a read on Rashad; his comments could fluctuate between amused and caustic, often within moments. Whether the man was kidding, Rolly couldn't say.

"Do we wear the chains we forged in life, Roland?" Huey reflected. "Does the accumulation of our misdeeds drag us down to eternal punishment in the spirit world?"

Rolly didn't recognize the reference—it was something from a Christmas movie, he knew that—but it sounded true to him. "Yeah. But karma doesn't wait until we die for punishment. It comes in this life, too, if we don't balance out the good with the bad."

Huey nodded approvingly as he walked around the GTO again and admired its sleek lines. He trailed a meaty index finger around the hood, then stopped by the driver's side door. "I, for one, believe we make our own destinies. As for spirits, I will leave those questions to philosophers and preachers."

"Well said, boss," Brad agreed.

Huey glowered at him. "Nobody likes a yes-man."

"Right, boss. I mean, ahem." The thief gestured to the stolen SUV he'd arrived in, an afterthought to the GTO parked next to it. "Let's talk payment. As this is the most expensive car we've boosted, how about a bonus? If the Lexus isn't spoken for, I was thinking you might—"

This time, Huey made no overt gesture to silence Brad; there was an unvoiced command in the boss's tilted head, the way his

mouth compressed into a hard line. "That is one of your problems, Bradley. Thinking. Leave that to me." Huey poked a finger
into Brad's chest, indenting the quirky T-shirt. "Even your shirt is
wrong. *Pi is better than cake,* eh? Have you ever had a cheesecake
from Junior's in Brooklyn?"

Brad took a small step backwards, his head down. "No. It's a
joke, boss. Pi isn't pie, it's pi. I mean, it's an irrational number
that goes on forever and never repeats, not something you put in
an oven."

Rolly felt the tension in the room jump, a sparking electric
current with Huey the live wire and Brad standing in a puddle of
water, ready to grasp it. Rashad, still fiddling with the GTO's
closed trunk, was whistling a tune that Rolly couldn't place, a
man unconcerned and unconnected to what was happening a
few feet away.

Spanish Ladies, Rolly realized. The song Captain Quint sang in
Jaws the night before he was bitten in half. The whistling sent
chills down Rolly's spine.

Huey's eyes were as lifeless as a doll's, though Rolly couldn't
quite tell if they were as black as a great white shark's. "I know
what pi is, Bradley. It is the circumference of a circle divided by
the diameter. I was making a joke, lad."

Brad let out the breath he'd been holding in, then forced a
laugh. "Good one, boss. I wasn't quick enough on the uptake."

"In addition to our arrangement, you and Roland may have
the Lexus," Huey said. "We will, of course, charge the standard
fee for clean plates and new keys."

Brad whopped in delight, and Rolly relaxed. While waiting for
their prize, they'd take their own rattletrap Camry to San
Antonio and cruise the old neighborhoods, reliving the glory
days. Though the orphanage was gone, an entire city block torn
down and gentrified by the influx of well-to-do Californians
snatching up cheaper property, it would do his soul well. And
there was the haunted railway and the not-so-small matter of
proving to Brad ghosts were real.

Outside, a vehicle's headlights threw their shadows against the wall as it swung into the parking lot and pulled to a halt. Through the glass of a bay door, Rolly saw two figures emerge from a black SUV, one short and wide, the other tall and thin. Though it was full dark, the car thief instantly recognized a Lincoln Navigator. It was a new model, 2022 or 2023, and so black it swallowed the meager illumination from a streetlight.

Huey rubbed his hands together, Brad's pi and Junior's pies apparently forgotten. "Rashad, I believe our friends are here. Be a lamb and open the door. Bradley, Roland, take that car cover from the workbench and drape it over the GTO."

Brad and Rolly retrieved the cover and began unfolding it, but Rashad didn't move. Among Huey's employees, Rashad had a long leash that he didn't mind pulling.

"How am I supposed to open this GTO's confounded trunk with a cover on?" Rashad said in frustration. "What if there's something in here worth keeping?"

"We promised a GTO Judge convertible, not the contents," Huey said patiently. "If there is a treasure secreted in the trunk, we shall keep it for ourselves."

Rashad dropped his tools on a metal tray with a clang. "What's the point of covering the car to take it off again?"

"A little showmanship is a part of doing business," Huey said. "Roland, straighten up the cover so that it does not drag on the floor. Bradley, open the door for our guests."

The prize covered, Rolly watched as a service bay door began moving with a loud metallic creak. When the door raised, the tyrannical darkness outside spilled inward instead of the light spilling out.

Who were these newcomers, and what were they doing here afterhours? *Good God, are they hitmen?* Whoever they were, Rolly had the distinct feeling it meant trouble with a capital T. He raised his hand to this chest, searching for the familiar amulet, then remembered. It was still hanging from the rearview mirror of the GTO.

Huey said, "Welcome, Judge Gantry."

Beneath the garage's lights, the short and wide figure resolved into a middle-aged man in a three-piece suit and alligator shoes. A gold chain hung across his prodigious middle and matched the coat's neatly folded pocket square, though the elegant proportions were spoiled by his bulbous nose and the overlarge hands protruding from his sleeves. The man was alternatively smoking and chewing a cigarillo, white horse teeth gleaming in a greedy mouth. Though not as extreme as Huey, he exuded a quiet menace beneath his civilized veneer.

Judge Gantry shook Huey's hand and said, "Gentlemen, this is my son, Abner. Say hello, Abner."

"Hello, Abner," the kid deadpanned.

Rolly laughed. The boy was tall for his age, about seventeen or eighteen, and looked as though he could dunk a basketball by standing on his tiptoes. He had his phone out, head bent, and wore the bored expression all kids had nowadays. Rolly would've thought Abner was adopted if not for the same horse teeth as his father.

Huey stood by the covered GTO with his arms wide, a carnival barker about to present the eighth wonder of the world to eager yokels ready to spend their dimes. "Judge Gantry, Abner. I present to you a rarity of rarities, the 1969 Pontiac GTO The Judge convertible." With a flourish, Huey whisked the cover off the car.

Gantry gasped, the cigarillo falling from his open mouth, its glowing tip coming to rest on his left shoe. Acrid smoke rose into the air, but Gantry stood motionless. For some moments, he seemed to have forgotten how to speak or even breathe. When he recovered himself, he rushed forward and said, "Huey, you've outdone yourself this time!"

Huey gave a slight bow at the waist. "What are friends for? The Judge for the Judge."

Rashad, not bothering to conceal his irritation, picked up the smoldering cigarillo and tossed it into a garbage pail. He went back to the GTO's trunk and renewed his efforts to unlock it.

"Abner," said Gantry breathlessly, "come look at your graduation present."

Brad leaned close to Rolly, his voice pitched low. "Who gives their kid a half-million-dollar graduation present?"

"Rich people," Rolly said drolly.

The fat man was dancing around the GTO like a *Fantasia* hippo in a pink tutu, his surprisingly light steps making no sound on the floor. His son shuffled closer, but the boy's hands were still on his phone, his head bent. Clearly, Abner wished to be somewhere else and couldn't care less about his new GTO.

Gantry didn't notice, or if he did, he was too ecstatic to care. He said to Huey, "Can we take The Judge for a spin?"

Huey clapped Gantry on the shoulder. "Patience, my friend. We will have new keys and a clean title for you soon."

"Before Abner's graduation, I hope?"

Huey said, "I will personally deliver it to your home that evening. The GTO will be waiting when you return from the ceremonies."

"You hear that, Abner?" Gantry said.

Abner didn't look up from his phone. "Yeah, thanks."

Huey's eyes flashed at the boy's obvious lack of interest, though his frown was barely discernable.

Rolly tensed; that was the look Huey had before Keith went missing. The chop shop owner placed a hand on Gantry's arm, the merest touch, but it was enough to stop Gantry in his tracks. The fat man ceased his effusive gushing, the glint of avarice momentarily leaving his eyes.

"Judge, please tell your son to put away his phone," Huey said quietly. "This is an auspicious occasion, but it is not to be shared on social media."

"Of course, of course," Gantry said with a quaver. "Abner, put away your phone."

"Hold on a sec, Pops."

"Abner, if you're posting any of this on Facebook..."

"Old people like you use that. Don't worry, I'm not posting *anything* about this."

Rashad was whistling *Spanish Ladies* again as Huey slowly circled the GTO, his expression impassive. Brad glanced at Rolly and nodded toward the door; if things got hot, they'd slip out the exit, payment notwithstanding.

Abner finally pocketed the phone and looked for the first time at the GTO. The horse-teethed youth was more of a cow staring incomprehensibly at something that had wandered into its pasture. He pointed to the GTO's front fender and said, "What's with the retro decals? *The Judge?*"

Gantry sighed. "The Judge is a special model of GTO; it was promoted in a segment on a classic TV show." Gantry went on for several minutes about a 1960s comedy called *Rowan & Martin's Laugh-In* featuring a sketch about a querulous judge.

Rashad stopped whistling and chimed in, "Does the boy not know who Sammy Davis, Jr., is? You know, *Here Comes the Judge?*"

Abner laughed. "Nope. Sounds like a dumb show inspired a dumb name. Pops, The Judge is a bit on the nose for you, isn't it?"

"Son, this car is for you."

The boy shrugged. "Fine. I'm going to law school after college, sure, but I don't want crap decals that look like they came out of a cereal box."

"Forget the decals and the show," Gantry said. "Look at *the car.*"

Abner looked, but he didn't looked pleased. "Hey, this thing has three pedals."

Rashad's mutterings grew louder, and Huey actually flinched. Gantry, jowls shaking with indignation, said, "The third pedal is called a clutch, son. Remember when we practiced on my Mustang?"

Brad muttered to Rolly, "Oh boy. Napoleon Dynamite is going to ruin this transmission in a week."

"If you can't find 'em, grind 'em," Rolly agreed.

Father and son sat in the convertible. Gantry was relishing the experience, his hands caressing the dashboard. Was he imagining the wind in his thinning hair as the convertible flew down the open road? Next to Gantry, Huey was chatting with his guests about the car's horsepower and acceleration.

Meanwhile, Abner was intrigued with Rolly's mass of lucky charms, still hanging from the rearview mirror. He interrupted Huey's remarks about the model's limited production number and said, "What's with the gold chains? Is this part of my present?"

Rolly stepped forward in alarm. "That's mine. I, uh, left it in the car on accident. May I have it, please?"

Abner took the amulet down and examined it. Beneath the garage's lights, the gold chains sparkled devilishly. "What the hell is it?"

"My good luck charms."

"Yeah? Do they work?"

"You can never have too much good luck, kid," Rolly said.

Huey was less than pleased at these interruptions. "Roland, take your trinkets."

Rolly retrieved his amulet, stepped away from the GTO, and placed his most prized possession around his neck. The gold was cool against his skin, almost cold, as it always was. With the amulet on, the shadows of Huey's Auto Repair retreated a bit, the spirits quieted.

"Reunited, and it feels so good," Brad said in his ear.

"You better believe it."

From the GTO, Abner's voice was a high-pitched whine. "What kind of entertainment system does this thing have?" In the driver's seat, he fiddled with the radio knobs on the dashboard. "Where's the GPS? The satellite radio?"

"That's a real radio, son, not satellite," his father said.

"Holy shit, there are no USB plugs in here!" Abner exited the GTO and slammed the door. "Worst. Present. Ever." He picked up his phone, talking over this father's protestations. "I'll be in the car, Pops." And with that, he disappeared out the exit and into the night.

"Today's kids," Gantry said sheepishly. "Oh, well. I guess I'll keep this jewel for myself."

"It's open," Rashad called out in triumph. He put away his locksmith tools and opened the GTO's trunk. Peering inside, he said, "What do we have here?" He picked up a sealed vase inscribed with a gold plaque at the base.

"What does the plaque say?" Huey asked.

Rashad tsked to himself and said, "My glasses are in my office." He handed the vase to Brad and said, "Read that inscription."

Brad took the vase. The plaque looked to be pure gold, the vase itself marble or quartz. Brad quipped that it reminded him of a giant martini shaker, but when no one laughed, he read the following:

> COUNT IVAN SKELETTY
> SEER OF ALL THINGS
> PSYCHIC TO THE STARS

Huey said, "It is an urn, not a vase."

Rolly gulped. "An urn? You mean there's a dead guy in there?"

"Correct," Huey said. "Brad holds in his hands the ashes of someone named Count Ivan Skeletty, who appears to be a soothsayer by the inscription. You did find the GTO at a funeral home, did you not?"

The vase slipped from Brad's hands. Rolly watched it tumble toward the floor, certain it would break. When it smashed against the concrete, scattering ashes all over his shoes, he felt certain his heart would explode. And that would be that.

In a blur of motion, Rashad dove to the floor and caught the urn inches before impact. He scrambled to his feet, said a few choice words to Brad about messing up his clean garage, and set the urn on a nearby workbench.

"Well, that would've been a mess, huh?" Brad said. "Mr. Gantry, I hope you enjoy your GTO. Rolly and me, we gotta run. After our payment, of course."

"Of course," Huey said. He nodded to Rashad, who disappeared with Brad into a nearby office.

Gantry slapped Rolly on the back. "Are you feeling well, son? You look as though you've seen a ghost."

"Gh-gh-ghost?" Rolly spluttered. "Why do you say that?"

"You look a little green around the gills," Gantry said.

Moments later, Brad and Rashad returned from the office. Rolly recognized on his brother the blissful look of a man who'd been paid in cash on a Friday.

The men chatted for a few minutes about the GTO before Huey called it a night. Rashad had to practically shoo Gantry out the door to get him to leave. Before driving away, the man had a long, last look at the GTO; Rolly half-expected him to blow it a kiss. *Good night, good night, fair GTO! Parting is such sweet sorrow, that I shall say good night till it be morrow.*

Brad was dividing their money, but Rolly hardly glanced at the bills being placed in his hand. *Count Ivan Skeletty.* Of all the GTOs in the world, they had to steal one with the mortal remains of the greatest psychic in generations, a man who communicated with spirits as easily as picking up a phone. And he was now a spirit himself.

A shudder ran down Rolly's body, beginning from the crown of his head to the tips of his toes. It was so strong he felt as though his bones would rattle apart.

"Rolly, snap out of it."

Someone was speaking, but Rolly didn't know who, nor could he understand them.

"Buddy, are you okay?"

The whispering voice was Brad. Rolly mastered himself and said, "Yeah, I'm a freaking Fredericksburg peach."

"What's wrong?"

"Do you have any idea who's in that urn?" Rashad had set the

Count on a workbench with no more concern than he would a carburetor needing to be cleaned.

Brad said, "There's no one in that urn; just ashes and ground up bones. Let's go home." He took Rolly by the elbow and started walking him toward the exit.

"Yeah, take me home." He'd stolen someone's remains! How in hell would he balance the cosmic karmic scales for that?

As the exit door swung open and the Dallas nightlife beyond beckoned, Rolly heard Huey say, "Rashad, dispose of that thing."

Rolly bristled. Dispose of it? That wasn't a *thing*. It was a dead person's remains; as such, it had to be handled with respect, not tossed in a garbage bin.

"Me?" Rashad said to Huey. "*I* didn't bring a dead body to work."

Rolly brushed away Brad's guiding hand and stopped. He wanted nothing more than to get away from this cursed chop shop and never come back; so why was he doing an about-face?

Huey's indulgent laughter was more chilling than comforting. "Very well. I will do it myself."

"Boss?" Rolly called out.

Huey said, "I thought you were leaving?"

Brad had one foot out the door. "We are. Y'all have a good night."

"Give me the urn." Rolly walked to Huey, wondering if anyone noticed how his hands were shaking. Despite his fears—or was it because of them?—he found himself saying, "I brought the damn thing here, so I should take care of it."

Huey looked Rolly up and down and weighed the car thief on scales only he could see. When he spoke, there was a new-found respect in his voice. "Roland and Bradley, you will wipe our prints from the urn, then put it some place it will never be found. It is evidence of a crime, and it must never be traced back to this place. Do you understand?"

Rolly took the urn and cradled it as carefully as a newborn baby. "We will, sir. Won't we, Brad?"

"Sure," Brad agreed, then muttered, "I've nothing better to do on a Friday night."

Rashad was crouched in the GTO's backseat and reaching for something under the seat. "Here's one more thing you two can get rid of." When he rose, he was holding two cards. "I found these on the floorboards."

Rolly snatched the items from Rashad's fingers, a vision of playing cards spilling out of a purse and into the wind. With a grimace, he remembered the woman who'd rushed out of the funeral home. "Rashad, when you picked this up, what positions were they in?"

Rashad scratched his head. "What do you mean? They were under the seat."

"Were they right side up?" Rolly asked. "Or were they reversed?"

Rashad thought a moment. "Right side up."

"What are they?" Brad asked.

"Tarot cards," Huey said with a dismissive wave of his hand. "Get rid of them, along with the urn." He bid them all goodnight, then went into his office and shut the door.

"You heard the man," Rashad said. He drifted away, attending to other duties before closing the chop shop for the night.

"Tarot cards," Brad mumbled. "Big deal."

"You don't get it," Rolly said morosely. "This card is the Fool. And God help us, the other one is the Tower."

On the drive home, Brad wondered if his brother's nut had finally cracked. Rolly sat in the passenger seat of their nondescript Camry, glassy eyes staring at nothing while his hands absently clutched the lucky charm necklace beneath his jersey. Count Skeletty's urn was perched in his lap, and the creepy-looking tarot cards rested on Rolly's knees. What had he called them? The Fool and the Tower?

"What are we doing with that thing?" Brad asked.

"You heard Huey," Rolly answered flatly. "We're taking him some place he will never be found."

"I mean, why are *we* doing that when it wasn't even our job? We were heading out the door, and you volunteer to dispose of some dead guy."

Rolly's voice was a razor. "Don't you know who this is, man? This is the Count Ivan Skeletty, Seer of All Things and Psychic to the Stars! Author of *Crossing the Great Unknown*."

"Never heard of him," Brad said.

Very carefully, Rolly set the tarot cards on the dashboard, then took out his phone for a quick internet search. Over Brad's objections, he read aloud the Wikipedia entry for background, then dove into more "trustworthy" sites treating psychic phenomena with proper respect. As far as Brad could tell, the Count and his daughter traveled the world, hoodwinked stupid people, and had more money than God.

When Rolly started reading the Count's obituary, Brad said, "Hold on a second. That girl from earlier, the madwoman who ran out of the funeral home. She must be the daughter."

Rolly stopped reading. "Yeah. She's an orphan; like us."

"Not like us," Brad said. "She knew her father, and he probably left her a fortune. Nice legs, but what was going on with her makeup?"

"Maybe she's a goth chick?" Rolly continued reading the obituary, his eyes bulging. "The Count's dying wish was to be buried in his GTO."

"You're kidding, I hope?"

Rolly's dry, audible gulp was an empty bucket bumping down a sandy well. "Listen to this: *Like the Egyptian pharaohs from whom he is descended, the Count will be accompanied to the afterlife by his most prized earthly possession: the ultra-rare 1969 Pontiac GTO The Judge convertible. The Judge, ever a balm to the Count's restless spirit, shall be his Chariot for the astral plane. Woe to any Fools who dared to disturb the Count's rest or his Chariot; may the curse of the Tower fall upon them.*"

"I guess you *can* take it with you," Brad said.

Rolly snatched the tarot cards from the dashboard and held them up. "See this one? This is the Tower."

Brad looked away. Somehow, the lightning splitting the tower's top and the people plummeting to their deaths turned his stomach to ice. He knew it was an ordinary card—an ancient card owned by a nutjob—but even so, he swatted Rolly's hand away and said, "When we get home, we're burning those things."

"The hell we are," Rolly said. "That would piss the Count off for sure, more than he already is. I bet these are from his personal deck. When he deals this particular baby, Whammy."

"Whammy?" Brad repeated.

"Whammy. Game over, man."

Brad said in a nasally twang, "Game over, man. That was my Bill Pullman imitation from *Aliens*, by the way. Hey, let's have an *Alien* movie marathon tonight. We'll grab some pizzas, get lit, and watch Sigourney Weaver light up some extraterrestrials. Phone home? I don't think so, bitches!" He mimed machine gun fire and laughed.

"How can you think of movies and food when we're cursed?"

"We're cursed?"

"You're not some innocent bystander in this story. You're as guilty as I am, and just as cursed. Unless..." Rolly's voice trailed off.

"Unless nothing," Brad said. "Put that stupid urn back on the floorboard. If we have a wreck, I don't want an expanding airbag to push the Count through your brain, though in your case it might be an improvement."

Rolly put the urn back down. "Pull over at the Walmart."

"Why? You want to watch the late-night freaks?"

Rolly straightened in his seat and braced for an argument. "We need some shovels."

Brad drove past the Walmart entrance. Rolly cursed and demanded they go back, but Brad refused. "We aren't returning the Count to that funeral home. And we certainly aren't burying him there. No way, no how."

Rolly was holding the lucky amulet secreted beneath his jersey. "As I see it, the only way we can avoid a curse is to bury the Count in hallowed ground. He won't have his GTO, but he might cut us a break if we give him a proper sendoff."

The little green vein in Brad's left temple was throbbing again. "A sendoff. As in, saying a few prayers and singing 'Amazing Grace.'"

"A song would be a nice touch," Rolly said. "You can't play bagpipes, by chance?"

"We aren't going back to the Shady Rest Funeral Home," Brad declared hotly. "If anything, I'm driving to a mental institution. A bit of valium, and I'll be right as rain. For you, a frontal lobotomy should do the trick."

Rolly ignored the cutting remark. "I'm not saying we drive him back to that particular cemetery. That would be too conspicuous."

"Right. And sneaking into some other cemetery in the dead of night with shovels wouldn't be conspicuous at all."

For the rest of the trip home, Rolly didn't say another word. When they arrived at their apartment building, he refused to exit the car or let go of the urn. Brad eventually gave up trying to talk him out of his ridiculous fantasies and went inside.

After an hour, Brad went back outside with two packed suitcases. He shoved the luggage into the trunk and jumped in the car, the smell of whiskey on his breath. "We'll bury the Count and the cards in some little country cemetery between here and San Antonio."

Rolly smiled broadly. "I'll say a prayer and you'll sing 'Amazing Grace.'"

"Done and done," Brad agreed. "Then you and I are taking a nice, long vacation."

Rolly wiped his tears with his jersey and said, "Brad, I know we don't believe the same things, and I know I'm not the easiest guy to live with. Thanks."

Brad muttered something about forgiving and forgetting, put the key into the ignition, and started the car.

Two days later, Brad Connolly was driving the Camry past the old San Juan Mission south of San Antonio, with Rolly in the passenger's seat. It was after midnight, and a rolling mist enshrouded the deserted, rain-soaked streets. Above, the lights of their hometown shimmered eerily against an overcast sky, while the searchlights of a business crisscrossed the clouds in a giant, double-looping infinity.

Despite the gloom—or because of it?—Rolly was in high spirits. His happy-go-lucky brother was back to his old self since laying the Count to rest in a nameless cemetery in the middle of nowhere. Beneath a moonless sky, the two thieves had dug a hole in a copse of live oaks, well away from the other gravestones yet within a decrepit picket fence. After covering the urn, Brad was eager to be away, but Rolly insisted they perform a ceremony.

Brad wisely kept his mouth shut as Rolly delivered a rambling, heartfelt eulogy that was half a prayer for the Count to rest in peace and half an apology for not including the GTO. When the eulogy was over, Brad sang "Amazing Grace," as he'd promised, all the while fearing the local yokels might show up with shotguns to question two strangers with shovels. But the lone witnesses to this bizarre funeral were some grazing deer and a red-tailed fox, and the men left the Count behind and continued to their vacation in San Antonio.

Rolly took a sip from a Whataburger Styrofoam cup. "Turn here."

Brad obeyed. "Stop drinking my Coke. Where are we going?"

"You'll see."

But Brad already knew their destination, thinking, *If you want to keep a secret, clean up your internet searches.*

"Pull over," Rolly said. "Kill the engine and the lights."

Brad parked along the desolate street of wooded lots and

abandoned businesses. Beneath a flickering streetlight, the infamous haunted railroad crossing strobed into and out of existence; Brad felt a migraine building at the base of his skull.

"These are the haunted railroad tracks at the intersection of Shane and Villamain," Rolly said softly. "I'm going to tell you a story, then we're going to do a little experiment."

Brad rubbed at the pressure building behind his eyes. "Experiment?"

"All in good time. First, a ghost story to set the mood." Rolly took a flashlight from the glove box and switched it on. He held the beam under his chin, pointed the light up his narrow nose, and spun a tale about a nun who, according to legend, was driving a school bus on this very street when it stalled one rainy night. To her horror, the nun saw they'd stopped on a railroad crossing and a train—one without a light or warning whistle—was barreling down on them. There was a mad dash to get the children off the bus, but time ran out, and the bus was cut in half. The nun was thrown clear and miraculously survived the impact; her charges were not so fortunate.

After waking from a coma, the nun was consumed with guilt. One stormy night, similar to the night of the accident, she returned to the railroad tracks, parked her car, and waited for the next train.

In the distance, she heard a train speeding through the darkness. She said her final prayers for forgiveness and closed her eyes, but instead of joining her doomed children, the car began to move off the tracks. The startled nun looked around and saw no one, though she heard voices behind her car, high-pitched voices that sounded familiar.

As the car's bumper cleared the tracks, the train thundered by and disappeared into the night. The nun exited her car, looking for the Good Samaritan who'd saved her life; all she saw were the smudges of small handprints on the back of her car. The ghostly schoolchildren had forgiven her and returned from beyond the grave to save her life.

As the legend grew, so did the story that the children would not allow others to meet their fate; if anyone parked on the tracks, they would push the vehicles out of danger.

"To this day," Rolly concluded, "local San Antonians and tourists drive to the haunted railway, park on the tracks, and put their vehicles in neutral. As did the nun's car, the vehicles move of their own volition—uphill, mind you—over the crossing's hump, and off the tracks."

"That's some story," Brad said. "And the experiment you mentioned?"

"I'm getting to that. Once safely on the other side, people sprinkle baby powder on their vehicles to better see ghostly handprints. Some visitors also claim to hear children's voices or see apparitions at the railroad tracks."

Brad knew the story, of course; he also knew it was pure hogwash. There was no evidence, record, or account of an accident of that nature in San Antonio; in fact, the closest analog was a fatal crash in Salt Lake City, back in the winter of 1938. During a blizzard, a busload of schoolchildren perished at a railroad crossing, an event that received national attention.

Why such a grisly story was appropriated by San Antonio, Brad couldn't say, nor did he particularly care. People were always repeating lies and hearsay and passing it off as truth; it was the birth of all religions, in his not-so-humble opinion.

"So, what do we do?" Brad asked.

"Pull up about twenty feet, to the edge of the tracks, and put the car in neutral."

Brad looked up and down the railroad tracks, as far as he could see in the darkness. The crossing had a flashing light to warn of approaching trains, but no rocker arm to close the tracks. He listened for a train's whistle, but the night was quiet and peaceful. Still, now that he was here, purposefully parking on a railroad track was the height of folly.

Folly. That turned Brad's thoughts to the Fool, one of two tarot cards they'd found in the GTO and buried with the Count.

The man depicted on the card had been strolling toward a cliff, as Brad recalled, without a care in the world. The precipitous drop the Fool was fated to take brought to mind the second, more gruesome tarot card, the one that had frightened Rolly to death: the Tower. Like the Fool, a man and a woman were falling from a great height to their deaths.

The words of the Count's obituary returned to his mind: *Woe to any Fools who dared to disturb the Count's rest or his Chariot; may the curse of the Tower fall upon them.* It was sheer coincidence the cards mentioned in the obituary had showed up in the GTO, nothing more.

Wasn't it?

Brad slow-clapped his hands. "You told a scary story, Rolly. Bravo. But that's all it is: a story. I'm not parking on railroad tracks."

"It's perfectly safe," Rolly said. "The kids won't let any car stay on the tracks; they'll push us off, I promise." He took a bottle of baby powder from the glove box. "Afterward, we'll sprinkle this on the car, and you'll see their handprints. That will prove ghosts are real."

Brad stared in wonder at his guileless friend. Years ago, a noted skeptic had demonstrated vehicles rolled off the tracks naturally, due to gravity. Though the road over the tracks *seemed* uphill, there was in fact a very slight decline. After safely rolling to the other side, the supposed handprints revealed by baby powder were nothing more than places where people had touched their vehicles and left behind all-too-human body oils. Case closed.

In preparation for this night, Brad had secretly washed the back of the Camry to remove any handprints. When Rolly sprinkled baby powder, there would be no children's handprints, only the tracing of Brad's index finger where he inscribed the message, *Ghosts aren't real.*

As fun as that sounded, some instinct was keeping Brad from going through with it. He started the car, switched on satellite radio, and tuned to a heavy metal station. "Let's get to the River Walk. I know an out-of-the-way bar with cheap drinks and cheaper women."

Rolly folded his arms. "Are you chicken?"

Metallica's "Enter Sandman" came on, muffling the distant sound of an approaching train; at the crossing, the warning lights remained dark, the bell silent.

Brad turned up the volume. "I'm no chicken."

Rolly began clucking and moving his head back and forth, pecking at imaginary grain. When he bent his elbows and started flapping his arms, Brad put the car in drive and moved toward the crossing.

"Do we stop here, Rolly?"

"Yeah, kill the engine and put it in neutral."

"Okay." On the tracks, with the engine and radio off, Brad put the car in neutral and waited for it to roll on its own. Nothing happened. To their left, a distant light cut the darkness, followed by a train's horn.

"Rolly?"

"I see it."

Brad felt sweat pop out on his brow. The train was still a good distance away; they had plenty of time to roll off the track, down the imperceptible decline. So why wasn't gravity doing its job?

"Why aren't we moving?" Rolly was saying. "These kids are supposed to push the car."

"Screw gravity and screw these ghosts," Brad said. Still in neutral, he turned the key in the ignition. With a sickening terror, they heard the engine splutter and die; meanwhile, the train's horn became a sound that filled the entire world.

Rolly was shouting for Brad to get out of the car, but Brad couldn't move his legs. He had a death grip on the steering wheel and the key, continually turning it, over and over, flooding the engine.

They were going to die; Brad knew that with certainty. A lifetime of regrets flashed through his mind, culminating into one overpowering thought: *I have killed my best friend.*

"Brad! Get out, man!"

I'm sorry, Rolly. I'm sorry for making you steal The Judge. Count, you're killing two Fools, when you should be punishing me. I'd make it right if you saved us, but it's too late.

The car began to move forward.

"The kids!" Rolly said.

Ever so slowly, the Camry rolled over the tracks and down the other side; inches from the bumper, the train roared past, an unstoppable and uncaring leviathan, then vanished into the night.

When silence settled on the haunted railroad tracks, only then did the two men find the courage to exit the vehicle, their legs wobbly. Behind the Camry, Rolly took his baby powder in shaking hands and sprinkled the car liberally, making sure he didn't miss an inch. Then he flicked on the flashlight.

"I don't see any handprints," Brad breathed. He had his hands on his knees and was bent over, blowing hard.

"Me neither."

"I have a confession to make, Rolly; I knew we were coming here, so I washed the car earlier."

"Why?" Rolly asked.

"To remove any existing handprints," Brad said. "That's what people find, not the prints from ghosts. In fact, if you look on top of the trunk, you'll see a little joke I wrote with my fingertip."

Rolly pointed his flashlight at the trunk. "Where?"

Brad stared at the flashlight's beam. He was certain he'd written *Ghosts aren't real* in the center, but the trunk was pristine.

Rolly was on his knees near the bumper. "Look here."

Brad looked. Clearly visible on the bumper were two handprints...*an adult's handprints.*

A crazy thought crashed through Brad's rationality with the force of a runaway train: Count Ivan Skeletty, Seer of All Things and Psychic to the Stars, had heard his prayer and pushed them off the tracks. Brad felt himself go weak in the knees, and he would've fallen if Rolly hadn't grabbed his arms.

"Easy," Rolly said. He led his brother back to the car's front seat and eased him down. "If you washed the car, who made these prints? Not a kid, that's for sure." He looked at Brad expectantly, waiting, the answer clearly written in his eyes.

Brad put his head in his hands, his mind reeling as he tried to process this gut-wrenching change to his reality. All these years, Rolly had been right and he'd been wrong. He thought, *There are more things in heaven and earth, Neil deGrasse Tyson, than are dreamt of in your philosophy*. The laugh in Brad's dry throat became a cough, and he took a sip of his still ice-cold Coke. "God bless Whataburger and their Styrofoam cups," Brad said.

Rolly put his hands on his hips. "Is that all you have to say?"

Brad gritted his teeth. He blurted out, "Ghosts are real." He glanced at his brother, waiting for him to launch into a derisive, triumphant tirade.

Rolly placed a hand on Brad's shoulder. "I know. And now you know it too."

Brad rose to his feet. "That's it?"

"That's it," Rolly said. He looked back at the railroad crossing, his brow furrowed. "The nun's ghost pushed us off the tracks, not the kids. Either way, I guess we aren't cursed after all."

Brad stalked back to the handprints. He bent down, daring to touch one with a trembling, tentative fingertip. The Count's curse was still on them, he realized. Tonight was nothing more than a temporary reprieve until they rebalanced the karmic scales. "We're going back to Dallas tonight."

"What about our vacation? We have reservations at the Hilton for three more nights."

"Vacation's over," Brad said. "We have a GTO to steal before that snot-nosed Abner gets his hands on it."

Rolly raised his hands. "Back up, brother. We're stealing the GTO? *From Huey?*"

"We'll iron out the details later," Brad said. "First, we're returning to the little country cemetery for Count Ivan Skeletty."

***

Sitting in a stolen Cadillac, Rolly raised a pair of binoculars and Judge Gantry's multimillion-dollar home leaped into view. The McMansion squatted like a puffy, ostentatious toad in this hilly suburban neighborhood undergoing gentrification. Similar homes were being built up and down the street, though none as grandiose. Some might have called it progress; Rolly had another name for it.

Up the hill, the GTO was parked at the top of a long driveway, top down. The convertible looked less lustrous amid the gaudy modernity of Gantry's home, with its stucco walls, satellite dishes, stained glass windows, and nude statuary forever pouring water into a marble fountain.

Rolly frowned; not only did the GTO not belong to Gantry, it didn't belong in this garish place. "What's the word where there's something that doesn't belong in time?"

"In time?" Brad said.

"Yeah. Say we went back in time to 1969, and we found a GTO with a phone charger."

Brad thought a minute. "Anachronism."

"Anachronism," Rolly said. "That's the GTO; it shouldn't be here, with these people." The car had a huge red ribbon tied around it, a half-million-dollar present for Abner Gantry's high school graduation. The family was at the ceremony, but an army of decorators, caterers, and waiters were industriously setting up in the backyard for one hell of a party.

Brad readjusted his enormous sunglasses and a phony beard, his fingers drumming anxiously on the steering wheel of a stolen car they'd parked down the street from their target. The disguise looked ridiculously fake, more so than Rolly's toupee and walrus moustache. Each man had ditched their normal attire for polo shirts, khaki pants, and topsiders—what they thought well-to-do people might wear to a summer graduation party.

"What else do you see?" Brad asked.

Rolly refocused the binoculars. "I see guys unloading kegs of beer from a truck, a caterer pushing a cart, and some lady with a computer tablet yelling at everyone."

Brad scratched at red welts forming along his wrists. "Damn these latex gloves."

"A rash is better than leaving our fingerprints in this Cadillac," Rolly said. They'd swiped the Caddy from a mall parking lot earlier that day with the intention of leaving it behind; the GTO itself would be the getaway car, if all went according to plan.

Brad asked for the binoculars, a frown forming beneath his crooked beard as he looked through them. "The setup's no good; Gantry's is crawling with people and guests will arrive soon. We should come back another time, at night. Or better yet, follow Abner until he parks it somewhere."

"I won't let that over-privileged, unappreciative punk kid grind up the gears because he can't drive a stick," Rolly declared. "His pimply ass behind the wheel would sully The Judge."

Brad lowered his sunglasses. "Sully?"

"What? That's the proper word."

Brad shrugged. "Yeah; I didn't expect you to use it correctly."

"Jerk." Rolly looked to the backseat and said, "What do you think, Count? Are we good to go?" He addressed these questions to a poorly wrapped present tied with ribbons and strapped into a seatbelt as if it were a person. If anyone asked, Brad was Gantry's cousin from Montana and Rolly was his partner; they weren't on the guest list because they wanted to surprise Abner with a special gift.

"It was a mistake to bring the Count," Brad said for the umpteenth time. "He'd be safer back in the hotel." They'd cleared their meager possessions from their apartment and put them in storage, in case Huey or the police caught their trail.

"And leave the ultimate good luck charm behind?" Rolly said incredulously. "I don't think so. With the Count, nothing and nobody can stop us. Not even Huey."

Brad winced at the name. "Then why didn't we steal the GTO

from Huey's? It would've been easier than this."

"I told you: there's too much bad juju at Huey's."

Brad swore. "Stop saying his name."

"Is he the devil? Will saying his name summon him?"

"If the Count brings good luck, that man brings bad," Brad said.

He believes in luck, Rolly thought. Since that fateful night at the haunted railway, Brad was a changed man. Having discovered the world was much stranger than he'd ever imagined, he was skittish, less self-assured. He'd even borrowed a few of Rolly's good luck charms, worn under his shirt. At present, he was gripping a trinket blessed by a reclusive monk who lived in a cave yet had an Etsy business and an internet connection.

"Indulge me, will you?" Brad said. "It was bad enough watching the boss deliver the GTO. We're damned lucky he didn't recognize us."

Rolly shivered at the memory. Thirty minutes ago, Huey had dropped off Abner's prize, no doubt with new keys and a spotless title. The delivery made, an Uber took Huey directly past their Cadillac without a second look.

"It'll be over soon," Rolly said. "We secretly drop the Count and his GTO in front of Audra Skeletty's house. Then we blow town forever, curse lifted, karmic balance restored, and case dismissed." Rolly banged down an imaginary gavel for emphasis.

"If someone asks what's in the box, what do I say?" Brad asked.

"There won't be time for anyone to ask; I'll pop the hood, connect the wire, and with my trusty screwdriver placed at the right spot, the car starts and we're out of here."

"But all these people," Brad protested.

Rolly snapped his long fingers. "Put me in that movie, *Gone in 60 Seconds*, and they'll have to change the name to *Gone in 20 Seconds*. That's how quick it'll be." He grabbed his hotwire and screwdriver and said, "Let's go."

***

For Brad, the walk up the meandering concrete path to the Gantry residence was a million miles long. Despite Rolly's assurances of good fortune, the haunted railroad tracks had turned every day since into Friday the thirteenth. Until the Count's curse was lifted, there'd be no peace for his troubled mind.

The old Brad's gone, he told himself. *The new one better suck it up and adapt to the changes in his environment, or he'll go extinct.* Brad's world had shattered with no less force than a rogue asteroid or doomsday comet smashing into the Earth sixty-five million years ago. Was he a proto-mammal, adapting to the changes and surviving the impact? Or was he a dinosaur?

Casting the situation in a scientific context made Brad feel better; all the same, he carried the Count as cautiously as a soldier tiptoeing through a mine field. Beside him, a carefree Rolly strolled up the path, whistling through his walrus moustache, the outline of a screwdriver barely visible in his left pocket. With the toupee, the man looked as ridiculous as Brad felt in his fake beard and sunglasses.

"Stop whistling," Brad said.

"Stop worrying about me and worry about your lines instead." Rolly resumed whistling "Patience" by Guns N' Roses; not only was he off-key, he was deliberately louder.

Grumbling, Brad went over their story. *Hi, I'm Cousin Brian from Montana and this is my partner, Raymond. No, we're not on the guest list; it's a surprise. This? This is a vintage 1969 lava lamp for Abner's college dorm. Cheesy, yeah, but what do you get a kid who has everything? No, we'd prefer to check out this GTO instead of coming inside, if that's okay?*

They were almost to the driveway when Rolly said under his breath, "Ditch the gloves."

"Gloves?"

"Your latex gloves. Take them off."

Brad thrust the Count into Rolly's hands, shoved the gloves into a pocket, then took back the present. His hands were fire-engine red, his fingers puffy sausages.

Beside the GTO, Rolly and Brad stopped and nonchalantly inspected the car. Caterers in white aprons paused while unloading a van nearby, their expressions neither curious nor accusatory, and returned to their work. The disguises, as absurd as they were, had at least passed a cursory inspection.

And why should anyone worry about two guys with a gift? Brad wondered. He was feeling better now that they were standing so close to their goal. *This is a party, and I'm Cousin Brian with a kitschy lava lamp for a trust-fund baby going to college, then law school, who'll meet some sorority sister and raise horse-teethed babies who can't drive sticks.*

"Are you ready?" Brad asked.

"Ready."

"Let's do it."

Rolly was reaching into his pockets for the hotwire and screwdriver when a voice said, "Who are you three?"

Brad turned to see the woman with the computer tablet, the one who appeared to be in charge. Viewed closer up, she was pleasingly plump and middle-aged, more handsome than pretty. With the tilt of her head and her darting eyes, she reminded Brad of a peacock. Rimless glasses rested above her beak of a nose, and she stared at them expectantly.

If she's seeing three men, Brad thought, *she needs a new prescription.* "I'm Abner's cousin," Brad began haltingly. He shifted from foot to foot and tried to recall his lines, but the words had flown from his mind, and he couldn't remember his real name, much less his fake one.

"He's Cousin Brian from Montana," Rolly threw in.

"From Montana," Brad repeated.

"I'm Raymond."

Brad stuck a thumb at Rolly and said, "He's Raymond. And you are?"

"I'm Janice East, the head of Judge Gantry's security team."

Brad blanched, but Rolly smoothly took over the conversation.

He explained how their plans had changed and they'd decided to come anyway, unannounced, as a surprise for dear Cousin Abner.

"May I take your gift?"

Janice reached for the Count, but Brad held the box closer and said, "I can manage."

"Of course." She shifted her bird-eyes behind Brad and said, "And who might you be, sir?"

"Huey."

The blood in Brad's veins turned to ice; beside him, Rolly's face was carved marble. *I told you not to say his name,* Brad thought. *Now he's here, Satan popping up in a cloud of smoke and brimstone.* Brad held the Count closer and said a prayer to any god who'd listen.

Huey stepped between them, expressionless as always. In the full light of day, his midnight suit gleamed dully, a horseless black knight in a suit of armor. He didn't look at either man, but instead took the woman's hand and said, "I was here earlier. I left without giving you the extra keys."

The bird-woman removed her glasses for a better look. "Oh yes, I remember you." She reluctantly took her hand from Huey's grasp and slipped the GTO's keys into a bulging purse that looked more like a weapon. "You brought this beautiful car."

Four heads swiveled to the shining, polished GTO. In the afternoon sun, every surface sparkled, from the windshields to the tires, and to Brad it had the intoxicating scent of freshly cleaned leather. Despite the gargantuan red bow tied around it, The Judge looked wretched, a dog forced to wear a choking collar that it hated and couldn't remove.

"Beautiful car," Brad heard himself saying.

Huey turned to him. "Indeed. This is a 1969 GTO The Judge convertible." The big man walked around the car, his hand hovering a fraction of an inch above the surface. "Pontiac made just one hundred and seven models."

"One hundred and eight," Brad said.

Huey arched an eyebrow. "Cousin Brian from Montana knows

his cars." He looked both men up and down, taking their measure. "Are you gentlemen car aficionados?"

"We are," Rolly answered. "Cousin Abner must be a special young man to deserve such a gift." He peered into the GTO with a casual air. "All original equipment, I see, and a genuine AM/FM radio. It's perfect, exactly the way it is."

"Too bad it won't stay that way," Janice said.

Huey looked up sharply. "What do you mean?"

Janice stepped closer to Huey. "You didn't hear it from me," she said with a conspiratorial air, "but I heard Abner arguing with Judge Gantry before they left. That kid is hell-bent on ripping out the radio and putting in a heads-up entertainment interface, complete with USB ports."

Rolly crossed himself. "Mother of God, *that* would be a crime."

"That's not the worst of it, young man." Janice bent her beak-nose to The Judge decal near the front bumper, a fingertip following the curve of the letters. "Abner will scrape off The Judge's original decals, paint the whole thing purple for TCU, and add a giant horned frog spanning the hood, sides and trunk. Stick around, and maybe he'll take you for a ride; he's promised to take people hot-rodding after the party."

Brad nearly laughed. Under Abner's tender ministrations, The Judge would become a giant purple joke with a ruined transmission. "Damn shame. Isn't it, Huey?"

The big man placed his hands together and cracked his knuckles like gunshots. "Janice, my Uber is waiting. Please give the Gantry family my regards."

Huey's cowboy boots rumbled down the path, but Janice fluttered after him and took his arm. "You'll miss one hell of a party if you leave." She rattled off a list of hors d'oeuvres and dinner options, ending with the fully stocked open bar.

Beneath the woman's beaming gaze, Huey's face softened a fraction. He took out his phone and sent away his waiting Uber. "I'd be delighted, Janice."

"Are you sure?" Brad asked. At Huey's scowl, he added hastily,

"What I mean is, do you want to stick around and see Abner and his friends driving The Judge?"

Huey studied their faces, a light of recognition seeming to flicker in his eyes. Beneath that withering gaze, Brad felt the sun baking his fake beard; beside him, Rolly fidgeted under the drooping walrus moustache and toupee. "Cousin Brian, Cousin Raymond, will you join me at the bar for a drink? We can chop shop."

"*Ch-ch-chop* shop?" Brad stammered.

Huey shook his head. "You misheard me, Cousin Brian. I said *talk* shop."

"If it's all the same to you," Rolly said unperturbed, "we'll admire The Judge a bit more, before it's ruined."

"Suit yourselves." As Janice escorted Huey to the backyard, he said, "My dear, have you thought of getting contacts?"

The woman folded her glasses into her gigantic purse. "As long as you're close enough, my eyes are fine."

"We'll see you at the bar," Rolly called after them.

Huey and Janice vanished around the corner of the Gantry mansion. In the backyard, a band could be heard tuning their instruments.

"He knows," Brad hissed.

"You're imagining things." The caterers had finished unloading their wares, leaving them alone with the GTO.

Finally.

In a flash, Rolly had the hotwire and screwdriver in his slender hands and was raising the hood. "Strap the Count in the backseat and take off the stupid ribbon. This baby's starting in less than twenty seconds."

With the hotwire connected and the screwdriver in the hands of a maestro, The Judge's motor sparked to life even before Brad removed the ribbon. The engine growled, eager to be away; it was the sweetest sound Brad had ever heard.

"Hey!" One of the caterers was rounding the mansion's corner, heading toward their cornucopia of a van. He was looking at the

GTO, one accusatory finger raised.

Rolly slammed the hood and got behind the wheel. "Get in!" Brad hopped over the passenger's side door and into his seat. Rolly slipped into first gear, and The Judge roared in approval.

Someone was yelling, "Thief!" and Brad recalled the Shady Rest Funeral Home, when a bedraggled Audra Skeletty burst out the doors and chased them before slipping to the pavement. He wondered if she'd be as pretty as her online photo when she found The Judge outside her home, her father's mortal remains behind the wheel and two stupid car thieves safely out of sight.

As Rolly put the pedal to the metal, gunshots rang out behind them. Brad looked back to see Janice, the pleasingly plump head of security, with a cannon-like revolver in her hands. Without her glasses on, she was firing much too high to hit anything but the hillside across the street. Beside her, Huey wore a roguish grin as the GTO raced away into the warren of Dallas's streets.

Brad took a deep breath. "We did it."

Rolly tossed his disguise into the backseat. "With a little help from our friend. Do you think they'll call the cops?"

"To report a stolen car as stolen?" Brad scoffed. "Huey would never allow that; we're golden, brother."

In the backseat, the wind whipped the rather poorly wrapped present, tearing off the ribbons, paper, and finally the lid to reveal a golden urn. Amid the awakening constellations of heaven, the spirit of Count Ivan Skeletty, Seer of All Things and Psychic to the Stars, smiled upon the liberators of his eternal Chariot.

BILLY DINKIN'S LINCOLN

John M. Floyd

Terrell, Texas
8:05 a.m., Tuesday, July 5

William Dinkin—Billy to his friends—had driven out of the motel parking lot and onto the highway when he saw the little girl flagging him down.

Billy was shocked, and a little frightened. His entire life—he was a single, middle-aged tax lawyer from Shreveport—had been one of structure and order and routine. Even this trip, a rare visit to a bedridden client who'd moved to Dallas the year before, had been boring.

Something told him that was about to change.

As soon as he pulled his powder-blue Lincoln Aviator to the side of the road and stopped, the girl wrenched open the passenger door and jumped in. She was blond and tiny, and looked to be around ten years old—eleven at the most. Her dress was muddy, her small body trembling like a leaf in a high wind, her eyes wide and scared and locked with his. "Help me," she said.

Billy nodded, and his mind cleared. "I will," he said. "You're safe now. Tell me what happened."

Breathing hard, she frantically told her story. She'd been walking beside the road when two men she'd never seen before showed up out of nowhere, grabbed her, and started dragging her toward a parked car she now saw behind a row of bushes. Terrified, she kicked and punched and bit and screamed and somehow got away from them, and—

"They're still out there somewhere," she said, staring through the windshield. "The bad men." She looked at Billy, obviously fighting back tears, and added, "I want to go home, mister. Can you take me?"

"I have a phone," he said. "We should call the police, right now."

"No, please—just give me a ride home. Our farm's close by. Two miles or so."

He nodded again. "Of course I will. You just sit still and rest." He cranked the Lincoln and put it in gear.

Minutes later she pointed to a maibox ahead, and a long gravel driveway beside it. Billy steered the SUV up the rutted drive to the house and around to the back, as directed. After parking, he looked around and saw no signs of crops or farming except one small, tilled area and a long, enclosed barn. There was also no car in the garage beside the house.

"Pa musta gone to town," she said. Then, in a pleading voice: "Will you walk with me to the door?"

He did, holding her hand and keeping a nervous eye on the woods and weed-choked fields as they crossed the yard. They were almost to the tiny back porch when he heard the screen door swing open and looked up, and—for a fleeting instant— found himself wishing for the boring life he'd led up until ten minutes ago.

Standing on the porch was a small man with a hard face and a big gun.

Dallas, Texas
1:30 a.m., Thursday, July 14

Mike Loomis, an employee of Huey's Auto Repair, finished

removing the doors of an '09 Ford Ranger pickup and stood up to stretch his tired muscles while one of his fellow workers started cutting out the windshield. The Ranger was being dismantled instead of being repaired because this was the hidden—and profitable—part of Huey's operation. Loomis and the rest of the night crew—they liked to think of themselves as specialists, overseen by a tough but fair-minded manager named Rashad—had riskier jobs than the legitimate daytime mechanics, but they also made more money. Which suited Mike Loomis just fine.

The windshield was done, and Loomis was about to climb in and start unbolting the seats when he spotted something in the adjoining bay. After a moment of staring, he put down his wrench, walked over to get a closer look—and stopped in his tracks.

The car in the second bay, still intact except for an unbolted front end, was a pale-blue 2021 Lincoln Aviator. Luxury rides weren't unusual here, in daytime *or* at night—part of Huey's sign out front said ALL MAKES ALL MODELS—but what attracted Loomis's attention was the almost invisible zigzag scratch on the Lincoln's passenger door. He knew this car. What was worse, he knew its owner: his first cousin Billy Dinkin. And according to a call the other day from his aunt Margaret, her son William had gone missing a week ago between the towns of Terrell and Mesquite, about thirty miles east.

After several long seconds, Loomis looked up from the scarred door, saw his bossman sitting alone in his office, and marched in without knocking.

"Rashad," Loomis said, "I got a problem."

After he'd explained things, it took less than two minutes for Rashad to locate the handwritten records involving the Aviator. As it turned out, the car had arrived at Huey's three days ago, delivered by regular supplier Martin Roberts, although both Loomis and Rashad knew that the name—like most of Huey's delivery contacts—was probably false.

"Where's he from, this Roberts?" Loomis asked. He'd taken a

seat across from Rashad's desk, but was too keyed up to sit still.

"Terrell." The two of them exchanged a look. "Might be a coincidence."

"You believe in coincidences?"

"Not really."

"What's he look like?" Loomis said.

Rashad frowned. "The times I've seen him? Short, maybe forty, going bald, dark bushy mustache." He tilted his shaved head a bit, studying his employee. "Want his Social Security number? Religious preference?"

Loomis forced a tight smile. He didn't mind the sarcasm. He understood that this was an unusual situation, to say the least. He drew a breath and said, "What I want is a few days off. Maybe a week."

"To find Mr. Roberts, or whatever his real name is."

"That's right. And find out if he killed my cousin."

Rashad leaned back in his swivel chair. No one was smiling now. "Maybe something else happened, Mike. Maybe there was a wreck."

"Car doesn't look wrecked."

"Maybe Roberts bought it, from somebody else."

"Maybe so. When I find him I'll ask him."

Rashad let several seconds drag by. Finally he said, "And if Roberts did kill him?"

Loomis didn't answer that. "Can I have the time off?" he asked again.

"I don't know. For this…That's a question for Huey."

"Why?"

Rashad hesitated. "Let's say this dude really did cause your cousin's disappearance. And let's say *you* cause *his*."

"That would mean Huey loses a supplier."

Rashad shrugged. "I'm just sayin'."

A long silence passed. "Is Huey here right now?" Loomis asked.

"I saw him out front ten minutes ago. I don't think he ever sleeps."

As Loomis rose to his feet, Rashad said, "Let me know what he says, okay?" Another smile crept in. "As I recall, you already had your vacation this year."

"Will you back me up? If it comes to that?"

"If he asks me what I think. Oh—one other thing."

The two men looked hard at each other a moment. "If you do find this guy," Rashad said, "and he did what you think he did..."

"Yeah?"

"Never show weakness," Rashad said. "Know what I mean?"

"I know."

Loomis found Huey standing alone in the moonlit parking lot outside the fourth bay, talking on his cell phone. He kept his distance, and after a few minutes Huey disconnected, pocketed the phone, and turned to face him. "What?"

"I'd like some time off, Huey. Till early next week, if you can spare me."

A silence passed. "I thought you went out to Vegas a month or so ago."

"I did. This is personal." Loomis took a minute to tell his story, in as convincing a way as he could.

Huey nodded slowly. "Your cousin, you say?"

"First cousin. My mom's sister's son. We played together as kids. He spent a weekend here with me last year."

When Huey didn't reply, Loomis said, "This Martin Roberts. Do you know him?"

"Not really, no. I have met him, is all."

"Good."

More silence. At last Huey raised his head and looked up at the quarter moon. In spite of the late hour, Loomis could hear what was probably the drone of trucks on I-35. He felt a warm wind riffle the blue shirt of his uniform.

"This is a business, Michael. Do you realize that? We have commitments, here. Deliveries to make, deadlines to meet. Relationships to protect."

"I know we do. But this is family, Huey. That comes before

business. At least for me it does."

The boss gave him a sharp look then, making him wonder if he'd overstepped. But then Huey turned again, and continued to study the moon as if nothing had been said. The wind had died down. Somewhere to the south, a siren wailed. Loomis waited.

"Do what you have to do," Huey said. "Be back by next Wednesday."

Loomis let out a breath. "Thanks. Rashad didn't think you'd let me go."

"Rashad?" Huey chuckled but didn't quite smile. "I am surprised he did not want to go with you."

Terrell, Texas
7:30 p.m., Thursday, July 14

Elizabeth "Lizzie" Barlow, the little girl who'd tricked the man in the fancy blue Lincoln into coming to her uncle's house to meet his fate nine days ago, was hiding in a stand of pines outside the Tall Texan Diner. The sun was sinking below the flat fields to the west, but it was still as hot as hell's waiting room. Her thin dress was soaking wet.

Her uncle—real name Bud Barlow—had suggested she watch the diner tonight instead of the motel just down the road. It didn't matter to her. She'd done this kind of thing half a dozen times now, sometimes the motel in the morning, sometimes the diner at night. Her assignment as always was to check license plates, and if she got lucky—if the plate wasn't local and if the driver was alone—she'd wait until the targeted victim left and hurry out to a point beside the road between here and the nearby entrance to I-20 (almost all vehicles with out-of-county tags were traveling the interstate) and wave the car to a stop. And the drivers always stopped; who wouldn't, for a kid?

Lizzie used her sleeve to wipe the sweat from her face, and a few hot tears as well. She knew this was wrong, and knew she hated doing it, but what choice did she have? She was ten years old, and Uncle Bud, sorry as he was, was her only living relative. Until she reached eighteen his so-called farm and his tall white farmhouse was her home, like it or not, and meanwhile she did as she was told.

Tonight's target, she'd decided, was a fat man in a white cowboy hat, currently chowing down in the diner beside one of the long side windows, a man who'd driven up in a brand-new Buick Enclave that she knew Bud would want to take to the chop shop in Dallas. She'd never been to the shop but she knew what they did there, and knew the cars and trucks Bud supplied them kept food on the Barlow table. Not to mention liquor in the cabinet.

Lizzie settled deeper into her little nest at the edge of the woods and continued watching.

7:45 p.m.

Mike Loomis leaned against the check-in counter in the lobby of the little motel a mile east of the diner, the motel that the Kaufman County sheriff said was the last place Billy was seen before his disappearance. Across the counter from him stood a uniformed desk clerk with a Sixties beehive hairdo and a Cruella de Vil scowl on her face. Adding to her appeal was the aroma of enough cheap perfume to choke a mule. None of this kept Loomis from asking her about the names William Dinkin or Martin Roberts or the physical description he'd been given of Roberts, but, as expected, she said she didn't recognize anything, and after questioning a second desk clerk who wandered in to see what was going on, Loomis decided to give up and book a room for the night. His current plan was simple: spend tomorrow poking around the town, mostly coffeeshops and cafes. Nobody'd said this would be easy.

After moving his car to a parking spot in front of his room and unloading what little overnight gear he'd brought, he walked back to the office and asked about a place to eat supper.

"Closest place is the Tall Texan Diner," Cruella said, without looking up from her copy of her magazine. "Just down the road." She pointed with a pencil she'd taken from somewhere inside the beehive on her head.

Hungry despite the lingering reek of perfume on his clothes, Loomis thanked her, climbed into his 2019 Honda Accord, and drove out of the lot and into the pancake-flat countryside. Off to the east, the moon was rising into a clear, purple sky.

The phrase *This is all a waste of time* kept repeating itself in his head.

7:50 p.m.

Lizzie was hungry too, not that it mattered. As she watched the diner, the fat man soon finished his meal, put his hat on, paid, walked to his car, and left. By that time she'd hustled through the trees to her position beside the road, and when the Buick approached she prepared to step out and flag it down. Just in time, though, she saw the headlights of a second vehicle approaching from the opposite direction. She stayed hidden in the roadside brush as both cars swept past her, her chance at the Buick gone. The other vehicle, she'd noticed, was a dark late-model Accord—a 2018, she thought, or maybe '19—and she especially noticed that just after passing her it turned into the driveway for the Tall Texan. It parked next to the diner's front door and a big middle-aged man in a work shirt and jeans unfolded himself from the car and entered the building. Lizzie heaved another sigh, returned to her former hiding place in the woods, and studied the new arrival's car more closely: the Honda had a Texas tag but was from Dallas County. Not far away, but far enough to be safe. Again, she settled down to wait.

***

8:25 p.m.

Loomis finished his chicken-fried steak, drained his glass of tea, and paid up. The meal had been fairly good, and about what he'd expected. He had the feeling small pleasures were all he was destined to get from this trip. But at least he was trying. He and "Blinkin' Billy" Dinkin had grown up together, and even roomed together at A&M before going their separate ways many years ago. Little had Loomis known he'd be the one to take the low road, but that's the way things turned out. The irony of it all— one of them an attorney and one a criminal—was something he'd chosen not to dwell on. He'd always suspected Billy knew what cousin Mike really did for a living, but if he did he never said so.

As Loomis pulled out onto the highway he saw a small blond girl by the side of the road ahead, and was surprised to see her waving him down. He braked to a stop on the grassy shoulder, and fast as lightning she hopped into the car, her blue eyes wide as goose eggs. Breathless, she blurted her name and her story.

After taking a few seconds to process this turn of events, he said, "They tried to grab you as you walked along the road? Right here?"

"Just down there a piece," she said. "But I got away, I sure did, and outran 'em."

He could believe that. She was small, but she looked fierce. "My question is, what were you doing all the way out here by yourself, at night?"

"My pa told me to walk to the store over there close to the diner, to buy some bread and beans for our supper. I sure didn't think nothing like this was gonna happen."

Loomis stared back at her for a long while. She seemed to have calmed a bit, and was gazing forward through the windshield as if they were already moving. It was full dark now, stars everywhere, and even with the car windows raised and the A/C purring, he could hear the chirp of crickets in the brush beside the road.

He took in a lungful of air and let it out. He was no psychologist, and damn sure knew nothing about children, but what this little girl had just told him sounded like the biggest load of bullshit he'd ever heard.

Finally he said, "Anything else you want to tell me, missy?"

"Lizzie."

"Lizzie, right. Is there anything else I should know, about all this?"

She looked at him then, and he saw her face change. It was as though she was surprised he even cared.

On an impulse he said, "Listen to me, Lizzie. I live in Dallas, and I know a woman, a good woman, who works for a place that looks out for kids who need help. You understand what I'm saying?"

"I guess…"

"What I'm asking is, do you need help? Do you want me to give her a call, about you?"

This time she said nothing, but now he saw the gleam of tears in her eyes. "No sir," she said finally—"I'm fine." Pointing, she wiped her face and added, "Let's go, okay? My house is that way, about a mile past them trees there."

He watched her profile a moment more, then started the car. Both of them stayed silent until they reached her turnoff, where Loomis steered the Honda past the mailbox and onto the bumpy driveway.

An empty one-car garage appeared. "Looks like Pa's not here now," she said.

Keeping an eye out for the two thugs the child had told him waylaid her earlier—he was still leery of that—Loomis parked out back as she asked, cut the engine, and checked his surroundings. To the left was a plain white two-story house; to the right a long barnlike shed and, beside it, a patch of recently turned ground. No farm equipment or vehicles in sight. As requested, he walked with her to the back door—but it opened just before they got there.

Standing in the doorway was a short, stout man holding a revolver—he was almost bald, with a black Grizzly Adams mustache. The gun was pointed at Loomis's broad chest. He remembered, too late, the automatic he'd left under the front seat of his car.

"So that's what happened," Loomis said to the man. *What a fool I've been.* "You're Martin Roberts."

"Who?"

"Where'd you get the name? Out of a comic book?"

The gunman studied him a moment. "Marty Robbins. I liked his songs. Who are you?"

"I work for Huey," Loomis said. "You killed my cousin."

As the two men stood there staring at each other, Lizzie walked silently past the gunman and through the back door into the house. Loomis could hear her footsteps on what was probably the kitchen floor.

He could also hear his heart pounding in his chest. The black hole in the end of the gunbarrel looked a foot wide. *Never show weakness*, Rashad had said.

"I don't know your cousin," the man said. "Who is he?"

"Was. He drove a Lincoln Aviator. Twenty twenty-one, light blue."

A slow grin appeared below the mustache. "I remember. A fine car it was."

Holding eye contact, Loomis pointed to his right, to the patch of new dirt in the distance. "That where you buried him?"

"Sure is," the man said. "Along with all the others. And I hid his Lincoln right there in that barn. Your car'll be there too, soon."

Loomis shook his head in disgust. "I'm not a good man," he said. "I know that. But I'm head and shoulders above you."

The grin widened. "Yeah, but I'm still alive, and you're fixin' to die." The gunman—Barlow?—cocked the revolver, the metallic sound sharp and loud in the quiet yard.

Loomis tensed, knowing his time had come. He knew he had

to do something, try something. But what?

At that moment he heard two blasts, one right after the other, and saw the man's chest spout a fountain of blood, and watched him pitch forward off the porch to land facedown in the dirt at Loomis's feet. In the open doorway behind him, holding a shotgun almost as big as she was, stood little Lizzie Barlow.

As Loomis's ears rang and his eyes stared dazedly at the corpse, Lizzie looked at him calmly through the blue smoke curling from the twin gunbarrels.

"I *do* have something I want to tell you," she said.

Dallas, Texas
10 a.m., Friday, July 29

Mike Loomis and Lizzie Barlow sat together on one side of a table in Huey's front office—the respectable part of the business. Across from them sat a pleasant, smiling woman with a briefcase and a stack of signed papers. For the tenth time, Lizzie squeezed Loomis's hand, and he squeezed back.

"She'll take good care of you," Loomis whispered to her, and sincerely believed it; he'd known Mary Watkins and her agency a long time. And the forty thousand dollars in cash he and Lizzie had found in her uncle's dresser drawer that night two weeks ago wouldn't hurt her future prospects any, either.

Huey, sitting in his dark suit and white shirt behind his desk ten feet away, looked pleased with Loomis and with the world in general, though it was hard to know for sure. Huey rarely smiled, and even a neutral expression like the one he had on today was a good sign. Beside him, Tish—Huey had introduced her to Lizzie and Mary as his "assistant"—was giving Loomis a strange look as well. Usually tough as old boots, this morning Tish had a glint of a tear in her eye and a tiny smile on her face.

The meeting, which Mary had described earlier as a "formality," didn't last long. Afterward, and after a few parting hugs,

Loomis stood at Huey's door and watched the little girl and woman leave. Twice, Lizzie looked back at him and grinned.

"Not bad, Michael," Huey said, watching them also. "You finally ready to go to work on cars again?"

Loomis smiled back at him. "All makes, all models," he said.

ABOUT THE EDITOR

MICHAEL BRACKEN (CrimeFictionWriter.com) has edited or co-edited thirty-two published and forthcoming crime fiction anthologies, including the Anthony Award-nominated *The Eyes of Texas: Private Eyes from the Panhandle to the Piney Woods*. Additionally, he is the editor of *Black Cat Mystery Magazine* and an associate editor of *Black Cat Weekly*. Stories from his projects have received or been short-listed for Anthony, Derringer, Edgar, Macavity, Shamus, and Thriller awards, and have been named among the year's best by the editors of *The Best American Mystery Stories*, *The Best American Mystery and Suspense*, *The World's Finest Mystery and Crime Stories*, and *The Best Mystery Stories of the Year*.

Also a writer, Bracken is the Edgar Award- and Shamus Award-nominated, Derringer Award-winning author of fourteen books and almost 1,300 short stories, including crime fiction published in *Alfred Hitchcock's Mystery Magazine*, *Ellery Queen's Mystery Magazine*, *The Best American Mystery Stories*, *The Best Mystery Stories of the Year*, and *The Best Crime Stories of the Year*. In 2016, he received the Edward D. Hoch Memorial Golden Derringer Award for Lifetime Achievement in short mystery fiction, and in 2024, he was inducted into the Texas Institute of Letters for his contributions to Texas literature. He lives, writes, and edits in Texas.

ABOUT THE AUTHORS

TOM MILANI's short fiction has appeared in *Groovy Gumshoes: Private Eyes in the Psychedelic Sixties, Black Cat Weekly, Illicit Motions,* and *Urban Pigs Press.* A good friend of Tom´s owned one of the early Plymouth Barracudas. After he sold it, he missed the car so much, he drove to the new owner's house to sit behind the wheel one final time. His experience made Tom wonder how far a man would go to get his first love back.

JAMES A. HEARN (jamesahearn.com), an Edgar Award nominee for Best Short Story, writes in a variety of genres, including mystery, crime, science fiction, fantasy, and horror. His work has appeared in *Alfred Hitchcock's Mystery Magazine, Mickey Finn: 21st Century Noir,* and *Monsters, Movies & Mayhem.*

STEPHEN D. ROGERS (stephendrogers.com) is the author of *Shot to Death* and more than eight hundred shorter works, earning among other honors two Derringer Awards (with seven additional finalists), a Shamus Award nomination, and mention in *The Best American Mystery Stories.* He's also a Distinguished Toastmaster who has performed stand-up comedy and led improv workshops.

JOHN M. FLOYD is the author of more than a thousand short stories in publications like *Alfred Hitchcock's Mystery Magazine, Ellery Queen's Mystery Magazine, Strand Magazine, The Saturday Evening Post, Best American Mystery Stories, Edgar & Shamus Go Golden,* and *Best Mystery Stories of the Year.* A former Air Force captain and IBM systems engineer, John is an Edgar Award finalist, a Shamus Award winner, a five-time Derringer Award winner, a three-time Pushcart Prize nominee, and the author of nine books. He is also the 2018 recipient of the Short Mystery Fiction Society's lifetime achievement award.

On the following pages are a few
more great titles from the
Down & Out Books publishing family.

For a complete list of books and to
sign up for our newsletter,
go to DownAndOutBooks.com.

Friend of the Devil
Crime Fiction Inspired by the Songs of the Grateful Dead
Josh Pachter, Editor

Down & Out Books
September 2024
978-1-64396-377-8

In *Friend of the Devil* editor Josh Pachter presents an anthology of stories inspired by lyrics from the Dead's thirteen studio albums and two of the band's many live recordings. Contributors include some of the finest contemporary authors of short crime fiction, such as award winners Bruce Robert Coffin, James D.F. Hannah, Vinnie Hansen, James L'Etoile, G.M. Malliet, Twist Phelan, Faye Snowden, and Joseph S. Walker. Also on board are *Alfred Hitchcock's Mystery Magazine* editor Linda Landrigan (with her first published story!), married couple Kathryn O'Sullivan and Paul Awad, Flemish writer Dominique Biebau, David Avallone (son of the legendary crime writer Michael Avallone), Avram Lavinsky and K.L. Murphy.

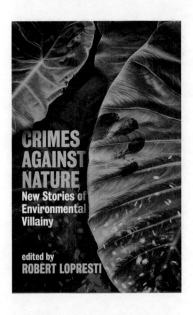

Crimes Against Nature
New Stories of Environmental Villainy
Robert Lopresti, Editor

Down & Out Books
October 2024
978-1-64396-380-8

The way we treat the world is a crime—fifteen of them, in fact. Some of the best and most honored mystery writers today have written new stories for this book dealing with environmental issues including pollution, wildfire, invasive species, climate change, recycling, and many more.

Authors include Michael Bracken, Susan Breen, Sarah M. Chen, Barb Goffman, Karen Harrington, Janice Law, R.T. Lawton, Robert Lopresti, Jon McGoran, Josh Pachter, Gary Phillips, S.J. Rozan, Kristine Kathryn Rusch, Mark Stevens, and David Heska Wanbli Weiden.

Scattered, Smothered, Covered & Chunked
Crime Fiction Inspired by Waffle House
Michael Bracken and Stacy Woodson, editors

Down & Out Books
October 2024
978-1-64396-381-5

There's no closing time for crime.

Editors Michael Bracken and Stacy Woodson order up hardboiled and noir stories by talented and award-winning crime-fiction writers.

Tales of redemption, revenge, and rebirth fill these pages, and each story serves someone (or something) scattered or smothered or covered or chunked. If Michelin rated crime (not food), the diners in these stories would all be three-star establishments.

You will never look at a roadside eatery the same way again.

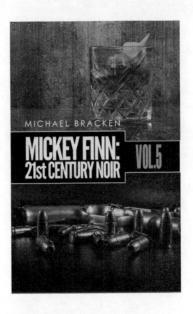

Mickey Finn Vol. 5
21st Century Noir
Michael Bracken, editor

Down & Out Books
December 2024
978-1-64396-386-0

Mickey Finn: 21st Century Noir, Volume 5, the fifth volume of the hard-hitting series, is another crime-fiction cocktail that will knock readers into a literary stupor.

The eighteen contributors, including some of today's most respected short-story writers and new writers making their mark on the genre, include: K.L. Abrahamson, Alan Barker, Michael Chandos, Caleb Coy, Eddie Generous, Nils Gilbertson, James A. Hearn, Hugh Lessig, Sean McCluskey, Tom Milani, Bill W. Morgan, Alan Orloff, Travis Richardson, Andrew Welsh-Huggins, Robb T. White, Sam Wiebe, Joseph S. Walker, and Stacy Woodson.